DISCOVERING JOOLES

ADRIENNE EASTON

AUTHOR NOTES and GLOSSARY

This story is set in Yarralinga, a fictional country town in South Australia in the late 1960s and early 1970s.

In writing this book, I have been reminded that South Australians have some sayings and words peculiar to them. For the benefit of those from other states, and indeed, international readers, I have included a glossary and notes.

Pub closing time in South Australia before 28th Sept 1967 was 6 pm.

High school years were referred to as First Year, Second Year, Intermediate or Third Year, Leaving or Fourth Year, and Matriculation (shortened to Matric) or Fifth Year.

School years comprised three terms of thirteen weeks, with a two week break for May holidays and September holidays. School finished a week before Christmas and resumed the first week of February.

This was a time when trainee teachers were bonded to the South Australian government. Study fees were paid by the government and trainees received a living allowance throughout training in return for teaching the same length of years as their course of study.

In 1966, Australia began an anti-litter campaign with the slogan, 'Keep Australia Beautiful'. This became a popular accusatory saying when someone dropped litter.

BATHERS. Swimming costumes.

CFS. Country Fire Service, a volunteer association of firefighters.

CUT CROOK. Be angry at someone or something.

CWA. Country Women's Association.

DINNER. The midday meal.

DUNNY. Toilet. Because of the scarcity of water, this was often a 'long-drop' rather than flushing. Consequently, it was usually situated some distance from the house.

GOING TO TOWN. What people would say when going to Adelaide.

GOING INTO TOWN. What people on farms would say if they were going into the local town.

INSTITUTE. In the early colonisation of South Australia, buildings referred to as Institutes were built in many towns to house libraries and meeting rooms for educational, social and cultural activities. They were used for community events such as dances, balls, concerts, lectures, film screen-ings, wedding receptions, and meetings for sporting clubs and CWA as well as doctors' rooms.

OP SHOP. An opportunity or second-hand clothes and knick-knack shop.

PE. Physical Education.

REACHING. An old English variant of 'retching' some-times used by South Australians of English descent.

SAPSASA. South Australian Public Schools Amateur Sports Association.

SMOKO. Morning or afternoon tea break.

SPOGGY. A sparrow.

STD PHONE CALLS. Subscriber Trunk Dialling calls enabled telephone users to make long-distance calls without going through an operator. They were introduced to Australia between 1962 and 1975. Initially, such calls were very expensive.

STOBIE POLE. A South Australian telegraph/power pole originally made from concrete encased in two steel I-frame girders. Named for its inventor James Cyril Stobie.

TEA. The evening meal.

THONGS. Casual rubber summer footwear. In some countries they are referred to as jandals, flip-flops, pluggers, slops or plakkies. Spoken of as a 'pair of thongs' or 'thongs' (plural) never thong (singular) which is underwear.

THREE-CORNER JACK. An invasive weed with sharp thorns which stab through thongs into feet.

TRANNY. A small, battery-powered transistor radio.

UTE. Utility. A Tilly in some parts of Australia. A vehicle with an open cargo tray behind the driver/passenger cab.

WC or WATER CLOSET. A room with a flushing toilet.

WOMEN'S BASKETBALL, BASKETBALL. The name given to netball until 1970.

PART I
JOOLES

Chapter One

Second Year High School, Spring 1969, YARRALINGA

'Grab us a coupla cold ones would ya, Jooles, and come an' sit a bit.' Dad always said it like that—'Jooles'—like I was some sparkly diamond necklace or something.

Funny the way he said 'us' when I was too young to drink. The 'royal we' my mum used to call it when Dad said 'us' but meant only him. Told us Queen Victoria used to say it.

Anyway, I didn't like beer. It made me think of the old guys at the pub who drank so much that they made thundering waterfalls in the dunny out the side. Nothing royal about that wee. Funny, but the pub was called the Royal.

Anyhow, Dad drinking on the back veranda on a Friday night—that was different. He only had the couple I brought him. Said it was his reward for the long week in the Yarralinga Garage and Farm Services. He'd sit there in his overalls, with grease lining his hands like black-drawn spider webs, take one of the beers and open it in the crook of his sinewy elbow.

'To ya health,' he'd say and clink his bottle against the sealed one I still held. Then we'd sit together, gazing out over the backyard—the tomato vines that needed staking (tomorrow's job) and the chooks fussing about as they took to roost—and watch the night creeping in over the fence palings.

'Nip in the air,' he'd say. 'Could be a late frost.' He'd gaze at his tomato plants like a protective mum watching her toddler on the slippery dip.

Inside, we could hear Mum cooking tea—fish it was on Friday nights 'cos Mum was Roman Catholic and a stickler for tradition. It was hard getting fish then, in our town, being so far from the sea. Sometimes, she bought it in bulk from Port Pirie and put it in the freezer, but when that ran out we had frozen cod from the shop, with barely any taste. She did alright though—dressed it up with white sauce and parsley.

Mum and Dad were high school sweethearts, but their parents had disapproved on account of Mum's family being Roman Catholic and Dad's being... well, whatever they were. I wasn't sure if they even believed in God. They sure didn't go to church. If you were Roman Catholic, you were expected to only marry a Roman Catholic. In our little country town, anyway.

But Mum and Dad convinced their parents and got married, and I was born just enough months after to stop the town gossips having a field day. 'A honeymoon baby' they called me, but from what Dad says, I was more like the honeymoon's-over baby. Life got pretty rough with me squawking and grizzling and driving Mum nuts. It was five years before they finally got around to popping out Patrick, and then the babies came thick and fast, one every year for four years. Then, whammy, the big finish with the twins... except it wasn't the finish, was it? Mum was right now trying to keep her big belly from bumping the frying pan off the stove.

'Julie?' called Mum. 'A bit of help, love.' Mum always called me Julie, never Jooles like Dad. She'd wanted to call me after some Catholic saint, but Gramma Kent put her foot down and said it was too foreign, and so I became Julie after Dad's big sister. Anastasia got shunted to second place and my initials became J.A.K. I would've liked to be called Jak, but no one ever took it up. Mum was pretty severe on people who called her kids nicknames, even Dad, but she must have gotten used to it because to him I was always Jooles. I think it reminded him of his sister who died of some strange illness in the year before I was born.

I looked up Saint Anastasia and found three. They'd all had hard lives and been martyred for being Christians. I was so glad Gramma had insisted I wasn't given that name.

'Julie!' called Mum, her voice rising on the final 'ee'.

Dad dismissed me. 'Go on, then.'

I reluctantly left him to his reward in the descending twilight and entered the Place of Great Noise.

Chapter Two

Mum's hair, sweaty from the frying, clung around her face. 'Check on the kids, will you? Get 'em washed up and at the table.'

Patrick, Sean and Conal had this wrestling thing happening on the sitting room floor, pretending to fall on each other from great heights, break legs or get totalled. It involved a lot of counting down and yelling, 'And he's out for the count!'

Aiden and James were leaning together on the couch—in the middle where the springs were saggiest—staring at the three older boys. James was sucking his thumb, and both had their blankies tight in their fists. They looked like they'd spent the day digging dirt.

I found my little sisters in the bathroom. Kathleen was sitting on the floor modelling for Maria The Hairdresser. Three of Mum's pink curlers were twisted into Kathleen's already curly red hair. It was hard enough to comb it out in the mornings (my job) without the tangles applied by The Hairdresser.

'Yoww!' yelled Kathleen as a pin went into her head.

'Sit still, Mrs Kent,' commanded The Hairdresser. 'You're going to look so lovely for the ball.'

The girls seemed like the easiest to move first. 'Gorgeous hair, Mrs Kent. C'mon, you've gotta wash up for tea now. Gotta eat, so you can dance the night away.' And surprise, they did. I didn't say it was fish. I left the curlers in, even though Mum would probably freak when she saw.

Then the boys. We had learnt this new word in biol about some soils: *aquaphobic*. That was the boys—they repelled water as if they were made of wax. But I finally got them to the table just as Mum was slapping dollops of mash on our plates and topping it off with a piece of fish and a splodge of white sauce.

I saw Mum do a double take when she saw the curlers, but I guess she was too tired to care. She said nothing, just kept ladling white sauce. Maria and Kathleen made disappointed noises when they saw the fish. But Mum and Dad were strict on that. 'Be thankful for the food we have. There's lots of starving people in Africa, and here we are with plenty.' Once, Patrick was cheeky when Dad said that. 'Then they can have *all* my spinach,' he said. He got a belting. So, when Dad made one little warning noise now, the girls sat up and smiled sweetly at him.

'Grace,' said Dad, and we all bowed our heads. It was Dad's concession to Mum's religion. 'Better cover all bases,' I heard him say to Grandpa Kent once.

'Bless us, O Lord, and these Thy gifts, which we are about to receive from Thy bounty, through Christ our Lord.'

'Amen,' we all said and fell on our food like the starving hordes of Africa.

The boys plastered theirs with Mum's tomato sauce. Patrick, who'd spent the weekend at his friend's place, said naively, 'The Atkinsons have Rosella sauce. Gee, it was really, really good!' Mum gave a funny little cry and stared down at her plate. Then she got up and went to the sink with her back turned to us.

'Patrick!' said Dad in his sternest voice, the one reserved for misdemeanours against Mum. Patrick looked up with wide eyes and stopped chewing so that the food made a big lump on the side of his face, like he had some alien growth. It made Sean and Conal giggle. I had to hold myself together, too.

'Apologise to your mother,' said Dad.

'Huh, um, sorry?' mumbled Patrick. I'm pretty sure he didn't know what he was apologising for. Patrick was a bit thick when it came to other people's feelings. I could see Mum lifting her apron to her face before she came back to the table. She nodded briefly to Patrick but was quiet for a long time.

We were all quiet, actually, with our heads down focusing on eating, until Conal suddenly laughed out loud and pointed to Aiden. Poor little guy was so worn out from his day outside that he had fallen face down into his mashed potato. Fast asleep! That broke the silence. We all laughed, and then, while Mum carted Aiden off to bed, we got back to the rowdy talking that usually accompanied our mealtimes.

Dad leaned across for the tomato sauce. ''Scuse my reaching,' he said, 'but I'm a bad sailor.'

I giggled, because that's what he expected, even though I'd heard the joke so many times before. Suddenly, Maria laughed. She finally got the joke. Kathleen looked at her and frowned. The boys went on shovelling.

After the fish and veg, it was time to fill up on fresh bread and Gramma Kent's apricot jam. Mum had sent Patrick, Sean and Conal down for the bread after school. But when she unwrapped the tissue paper, she found a huge hole in the end.

She looked at the boys.

The boys looked down in their laps.

She looked at Dad.

His eyes were twinkling. 'Seems we have a mouse problem, Fiona,' he said.

The corners of Mum's eyes were crinkling, even though her lips were pressed in a firm line.

'Mmm. I'll need to set a trap,' she said. She cut the bread and placed the first slices on the boys' plates. All their slices were rings of crust with nothing in the middle.

Conal slumped back in his chair and crossed his arms. 'Not fair!' he grumped.

Patrick and Sean said nothing and slopped jam into the hole as if there was bread there.

We all laughed then. Loud!

When we'd calmed down a bit, Dad talked about the farmers all wanting their machinery fixed, ready for what promised to be a bumper harvest, so he'd likely be working late at the garage for a while and could I help Mum a bit more with the kids.

'You look tired, love,' he said to Mum. 'Why don't you go and put your feet up. Jooles and I can see to the kitchen and the kids.' And even though it was greasy Friday washing up, and I really wanted to flop on my bed and read, I didn't grump. I could see Mum was worn out.

Chapter Three

Dad loved his garden. It was his space—certainly not Mum's. She ruled the house, if ruled is the right word. It was a division of labour of sorts—the house was hers and the garden his. You could tell a lot about them from the way they kept their particular areas. The garden, the shed, the lawns, the trees… everything was organised and trimmed and tidy. I reckon if you could see inside Dad's head, it'd be like that.

'A place for everything and everything in its place,' he'd say as he washed off the spade and the rake and hung them on the shadow outlines painted on the pegboard. He never left them lying around the yard or propped against the wall or spiked into the veggie patch like Mr Sullivan next door. Mr Sullivan had a nasty accident once when he trod on the rake prongs and levered the handle up into his nose. Broke it. Blood everywhere and the air blue with his swearing. Didn't change him though. I'd still see his tools lying around, accidents waiting to happen.

No, my dad was not like that. If anything, he was the opposite, a real stickler for tidiness, so I knew exactly where to fetch whatever he asked for when we worked together in the garden on weekends. It was his favourite space.

'Don't you just love the feel of dirt?' and 'Here, smell this, Jooles,' as he held up a handful of compost writhing with fat earthworms. 'Can't smell anything, eh? Lovely! Just how it should be.'

And the plants responded to his love for their growth and fruiting. Fruit, they did—more than we could ever eat, and that was saying something for our tribe.

'Here, Jooles, skip this down to old Mrs Watson, would ya?' he'd say as he handed me a basket of beans and cucumbers and tomatoes, or whatever was in season. Sometimes, if the recipient was Mrs Watson (not miserly Mrs Anderson or Mrs Hillman whose basket I left on the front porch because she never answered her door) some of the fruit and veggies would come back in jars with fancy labels in beautiful, old-fashioned writing—Dill Pickles, Tomato Relish, Plum Jam.

But Mum… Mum was different. I wondered sometimes how they ever made it work. He loved everything tidy and organised, while Mum… well, she loved people, and sometimes I think that she didn't even see the mess around the house.

'Jooles, have you seen my purse anywhere? One of the kids must have gone off with it.'

But they hadn't. It'd turn up between the lounge cushions where she'd flopped, exhausted, and then had to break up an argument between the kids, or in the fridge where she'd put it down because she needed two hands to put away the cheese among the shelves stuffed with beans, tomatoes, and cucumbers.

Mum went out a lot—CWA meetings (secretary), P&F meetings (vice-president), afternoon tea with friends (chief organiser), playtimes for the kids and their friends (those of us not at school yet). She was a social whirly-whirly that only came back home to cook and wash and sleep, but not to tidy or clean. That is, except when Dad sighed as he shifted yet another pile of laundry from his spot on the lounge.

'Sorry, love.' She'd smile sweetly at Dad. 'Haven't got to that yet.'

'Righto, righto,' he'd concede, swat her bottom gently, then ease his tired frame into the couch.

Granny Murphy took pity on Dad and came two mornings a week to help around the house. If it weren't for her, I think we'd have sunk under a growing forest of toys, laundry, decomposing apple cores and half-eaten rusks—the detritus of little kids. It's not that we had a lot. It's just that it got all higgledy-piggledy and we were snared in it, muddling along as best we could.

I was more like Dad. I liked knowing that everything was in order, and I could find what I wanted when I needed it. Being the eldest, I had the most space of my own—not a whole bedroom because we only had three. I had to share with Maria and Kathleen, but Dad made a divider of wardrobes and a curtain so that it was nearly my own room. No one was allowed to go past the wardrobes and step foot on the cotton rug (Dad and Mum's rule) so I could keep my space just how I liked it.

Not that I got to spend much time in my space that December.

Chapter Four

Dad rushed Mum off to Redbank Hospital on the seventeenth. They barely made it before Brigid was born. Dad got to hold her straight away and then have a cup of tea with Mum. Pleased as punch when he told us.

With the rest of us, he'd been sent home as soon as he got Mum there. 'Husbands are hopeless at times like these,' the matron had said as she shooed him out the main doors. But this time, he knew the baby was close and hung around. A nurse saw him and told him when Brigid had arrived.

'She's a corker,' he told us. 'Another redhead.' He looked at Kathleen and she glowed and sighed with delight.

I missed the last two days of Second Year because I had to stay home and look after the house and the twins while Dad went to work and the other kids were at school. It was fine. I was fine. We all were.

Gramma Kent and Granny Murphy helped a lot. Dad

cooked sometimes—sausages and eggs and chips. 'A bachelor's tea,' he called it. We loved it.

Mrs Price sent Em (my best friend) over one night with a whole roast shoulder of mutton and veggies. Her twin, Jason, followed with an apple pie and a brick of Golden North ice cream. Our eyes popped.

'Wow!' said Dad, a bit overcome. 'Wait there, you two.' He disappeared into the garden and came back with a container of the first ripe tomatoes. In Yarralinga, there was a competition to be the first to have tomatoes by Christmas, and I'd never seen Dad give those away before.

There wasn't much talk that teatime as we devoured the feast. Mrs Price had sent so much that, even with nine of us, there was enough to make us groan with full bellies.

A couple of days later, the boys hounded me to buy some bacon. 'Like the Atkinsons have,' said Patrick. I gave in, even though I had no idea how much to get or how much it cost. The butcher raised one eyebrow when I asked him for a pound of bacon. He said nothing, weighed it out and wrapped it up. I felt sick when he told me how much it cost but I paid and got out of there as fast as I could. I went straight home. There was nothing left to buy the flour and butter that was on my list. *How does Mum do this?* I vowed never to complain again about what we couldn't have. And I'd get stuck into Patrick if he whined or even mentioned what others had that we didn't.

Mum and Brigid came home after five days. I overheard Mrs Hawkins say to Mrs Vincent in the post office that it just wasn't right to come home so soon. *She'd* stayed the full ten days. It was what was best for all concerned. Mrs Vincent made agreeing noises, even though she didn't have any kids. Then they noticed me and turned away. But not before Mrs Vincent flushed pink.

I told Mum about it.

'Oh, the silly ladies!' she said. 'We're both perfectly fine. Brigid's feeding well and I feel great. Don't take any notice of them, Julie. I'm just so glad to be home. Thank you for all you've done.'

Mum gave me a warm hug. She smelled of milk and Johnson's baby powder. Life felt right again.

THAT CHRISTMAS, Gramma and Grandpa Kent bought a television. Grandpa fiddled around with the bunny-ear aerials to stop the screen being a fizz of snow while we stood around anticipating a beautiful moving picture. He swore softly a couple of times, but finally a picture emerged. Every now and then, people wiggled out of shape as lines ran up the screen. Like one of those funny mirrors at the Redbank Show.

No matter how much the boys whined about everyone else having one, Mum and Dad wouldn't give in. I reckoned we couldn't afford it. The boys used to sneak over to Gramma's and watch it. I did a couple of times. Gramma had hung blue cellophane over the screen because she'd heard that it stopped some kind of light waves from hurting your eyes. The boys thought it turned the black and white into colour.

Mostly, Grandpa and Gramma fell asleep with the cricket commentator droning on in the summer heat. Grandpa's head hit his chest and his false teeth dropped.

EMILY PRICE WAS my best friend, and I was hers—well, apart from Jase, her twin. They were really close. She used to say, 'It's a twin thing, Jooles,' as though she wanted to make me feel better when she spent some time with him instead of me, like playing tennis that I didn't play. It was alright, though. I was alright. I got it. It was a lot like me spending time with Dad gardening on the weekends. Or with Mum. She was my friend even if she was my mum. We could talk about anything. I felt sad for Em sometimes because her mum was not like mine at all—Mrs Price was sort of closed in on herself.

I don't remember a time without Em, without sitting next to each other in school, and weekends spent at each other's houses or around the town. People sometimes asked us if we were twins—maybe because we were nearly always seen together—which was pretty funny because we were so different.

She was dark-haired and her skin tanned easily. My hair was light brown and in summer I had freckles or peeling skin from sunburn on the bridge of my nose and cheeks. I was taller than her—not much though—and sort of rounder, while she was lean.

Em was fast and loved sport; I didn't love it. I played basketball in winter because she did and my mum and dad wanted me to. I played goalkeeper; Em played centre or wing attack.

Dad said I was patient and calm (not always with my brothers). Mr Price called Em a hothead. She used to get annoyed with me when she thought I was shutting her down because I asked so many questions about her ideas. But then she'd see sense in what I was saying and we'd meet in the middle, and it'd all work out right, especially with school projects.

We trudged through maths, plodded through science and waded through geography. But we both loved to read: English was our favourite subject.

I hardly got to see Em that summer because I was needed at home to help with the kids, or Dad in the garden. The times we did, often Jase and their dog, and sometimes Tom Lawson, came with us, riding our bikes around Crystal Lake to sit on the dam wall and skim or throw stones into the dark water. Sometimes, we'd join up with other townies and build forts in the pine trees, or ride down Memorial Drive where every tree had been planted for a fallen soldier, and out past the cemetery toward Elizabeth Springs. We never got further than Wilson's Crossing because there was a reed-ringed waterhole where we could swim or go yabbying. Especially in summer holidays.

PART II
EMILY

Chapter Five

January 1970

Grandad's house sat dormant over that long, hot summer. Our parents had our own garden to look after, so Grandad's quietly settled into a state of neglect. The fruit fell plump and ripe to the ground and rotted in the heat. The air was heavy with sweet fermentation and the buzz of drunken bees.

Grandad had died in November. He outlived Grandma by just five months. Their weatherboard house sat vacant. I asked my dad, who was the eldest and the executor of his father's will, 'Why can't we go inside?'

'We have to wait until Aunt Caroline comes home from America,' he replied, 'so she can help sort through what she wants. Don't want her or Uncle Bob accusing us of throwing out stuff they want. Or taking it.'

The house sat on a quarter of an acre on Railway Terrace. Grandad, who discovered the joy of gardening in his retirement, had tended a large orchard and vegetable garden from which Grandma made preserves and pickles, jams and chutneys. Bottles and jars sat row by row upon her pantry shelves.

Most of all, Grandma loved to be among her roses. They stood along the front fence, blooms fluffed and puffed like prize roosters or tumbling like playful children over the two arbours that faced each other across the rectangular lawn. That is, until winter, when Grandma could be found wielding her secateurs like an axe murderer, pruning what seemed to be the very life out of them—right down to a few hardy stems.

'Putting them to bed,' she called it. And sure enough, they'd awaken with the spring and reward her abundantly. She put roses in every room of the house.

We often found Grandad in his garden shed, shelling almonds. I think he liked the quiet—Grandma was 'a talker' according to Dad.

My dad had grown up in that house along with his younger brother and two sisters. There were seven of us cousins, but only four of us lived in the town by the time Grandad and Grandma died. Aunty Sue and Uncle Steve had moved their family to Adelaide before Jase and I even went to school. We only saw them at Christmas when they paid a fleeting, obligatory visit. Uncle Ken Carey and Aunty Chrissie, Larry and Tommy remained in Yarralinga. They joint-owned Carey's Grocery with my parents.

That January, we four younger cousins—Larry and Tommy, Jase and I—found ourselves flung together in a loose friendship, mostly because the kids that we usually hung around with had gone down to their family shacks by the beach to fish and swim. We were not of that crowd, our family being too poor to own a shack, and Dad was always at the shop—we never went on holiday.

Of those left in town, our parents were of the let-them-roam-free parenting type and were more than happy for us to be out in the darkness. We felt sorry for other kids whose parents made them stay in after dark. My best friend Jooles was one of them. Her mum had just had baby number nine, so Jooles was needed to help with the others.

We roamed the streets and invented games of intrigue, complete with unbreakable codes and operations that required stealth. We had the advantage of being slight in stature and dark-haired and that, with a deep suntan, enabled us to creep in the shadows and spy through people's windows. We saw that Mr Thomas, our headmaster, stayed late after the poker games at Annabelle Berry's, and she always pulled the blinds; the blue, flickering light of Crisps' TV shone out through the lace curtains; Hermann Schneider's huge rottweiler slunk out to the abattoirs and menaced the penned sheep; the obese cat that the Sullivans thought was theirs went down to the Patterson's every night and was welcomed as if they thought she was *theirs*; and Bob Smythe sat out on his front veranda drinking and smoking while his wife watched TV at decibels above healthy. He was a dim shadow under the vines, but we could see the red-eye glow of his cigarette. That summer Larry got a packet of his mum's Winfields and showed us how to smoke.

Our cousin Larry was a year older than Jase and me (we'd turned fourteen that January). His voice had slipped, he had a shadow on his top lip and was cocky when he was around younger kids. He usually hung around with a group of much older boys, and he told us the stuff they did but with the threat that he'd come in the night and suffocate us with our pillows if we ever told on them. They played one prank on Father O'Day up at the Catholic Church. He had two rabbits, does with pink eyes and pristine white fur on account of him combing them daily. Larry and his gang got a buck one night and put it in with them and then a month later there were all these little kittens! I remember Dad and my Uncle Ken falling about laughing at Father O'Day preaching on the miracle of the Immaculate Conception and his rabbits being proof.

Larry's little brother, Tommy, was only eight but, because Aunty Chris insisted we look after him, he had to tag along. He was a pain.

IT WAS near the end of January, and we were getting bored —no one in our small town seemed to do anything worth spying on anymore. A half-moon was trying to outshine the Milky Way and giving us plenty of light to amble toward home. As we came to Grandad's, Larry suddenly dared us to go inside.

'What? Into Grandad's?'

'Yeah, come on.' And he swung over the car gate into the drive. He had this cool way of leaping at the gate sideways, gripping the mesh and vaulting up and over. I tried it once but must've been too short. I was glad I was alone that time.

'No, Larry, we're not s'posed to,' said Tommy.

'So? They won't know. Anyway, it's not like we're strangers… it's our Grandad.'

'But isn't it breaking in?' asked Jase.

'Nah, it's not. It's our Grandad's, so it's ours, right? You comin' Em? Jase?'

Jase and I climbed over the gate and went up the path. Tommy gave up and followed, complaining, 'We shouldn't be doing this…'

'Shut up!' I said. 'Be quiet or go home!' He looked at me from under his shaggy fringe as if I were a witch.

We tried the front door. It was locked.

'Let's try the back,' said Jase and reminded us about the key on the hot water tank.

'Keep your voices down,' Larry warned as he nodded towards the neighbours. The sound of the Crisp's TV floated over the flattened-iron fence, and we could see pinpricks of light where nails had popped. We followed him down the side of the house.

It was dark on the back porch. My foot knocked an empty can. It rolled down the step onto the concrete path with a sound I thought would never fade. That set the Sullivan's dog barking at their back fence, and we held still until it gave a final mutter and was quiet. Our eyes were getting used to the deep dark by now. I turned to the back door and jumped and sucked in my breath. Then I realised that it was only a hat and coat draped on the coat rack with Grandad's rubber boots underneath.

Larry felt around on the water tank for the key, but it wasn't there—Dad must've taken it.

'So, let's try the windows,' I said.

Then Tommy surprised us. 'I know! The wood-box!'

And he ran to the other side of the porch and lifted the wood-box door, so it rested against the kitchen wall.

Jase said, 'Good one, Tom.'

Tommy's chest puffed out. 'I 'membered that!' he said. 'I'll climb through. I can fit.'

We pulled logs out and stacked them against the wall until we'd cleared enough room for Tommy to crawl into the kitchen. He opened the back door, and we were inside.

Had we ever been in Grandad and Grandma's in the dark? Without them? We stood still, barely breathing. It was close, warm, and stale smelling from years of roast dinners. We could hear the roof cracking and popping. There was a scrabbling sound from behind the fridge. That was all.

My hair crawled along the base of my neck, and I remembered being at school camp and having to go to the loo in the darkest night, way across this wide space surrounded by creaking trees. I shuddered.

Chapter Six

The moonlight shone underneath the half-drawn roller blind and across the kitchen table. A newspaper lay open on it. A vase held three dried rose stems; the petals had fallen, dead, onto the tabletop. There was a scattering of almond shells and a pencil. Grandad used to do the crossword.

'Arrrrrrrr!' said Larry behind us in a scary voice. We jumped and giggled.

'Hide and Seek!' he said, 'I'm He and this is Home.' He slapped the back door. 'Go!'

Still, we hovered.

'Go!'

And we scattered.

At first, by some unspoken, yet agreed rule, we crept to hide in the rooms that were familiar to us: the kitchen, the lounge and the hall. But as we hid and ran and tackled one another, tumbling in the dark and slipping on the hall runner, we became less mindful of it being Grandad and

Grandma's. It became our playground—our dark, cluttered playground—and we began to venture into the front rooms.

When at last, it was my turn, Larry failed to show. I'd found Jase easily. He always sneezed a lot in dusty places and there was plenty of it in the spare-room curtains. And Tommy… well, he was getting found first all the time, so I let him sneak to home base while I looked for the others.

But Larry didn't come out, so we went searching together and found him on the floor beside Grandad and Grandma's bed. He stood up when we came in and we saw then that the dressing table drawer was open. He held something that shone in the streetlight.

'Look,' he said. It was a gold watch, not one with a band to wear on the wrist, but with a chain to wear on a man's coat vest. I took it from his hands and smoothed my fingers over the decorative case as it sat solid in my palm. The initials WJB (not Grandad's but his father's) were engraved there in curling letters. It had a cover that sprung open to reveal the Roman numerals on its face. It was a beautiful thing.

'Me. Me.' I gave it to Tommy and turned to the open drawer.

'What else is there?' asked Jase and he pulled out a couple of dark boxes.

'Look! Grandma's pearls!' I lifted the strands from their velvet case and held them to the streetlight. I ran my fingers along their length and felt their cool silkiness.

We kept our voices to husky whispers as we exclaimed over the contents of that drawer: we were aware of something sacred. There were things our grandparents had worn, like Grandad's cufflinks. But then, there were things we'd never seen before, like a silver locket with faded photos—of whom, we didn't know. Some things seemed very old and expensive; others had been thrown there on a moment—bobby pins and unthreaded beads, a broken comb, stamps and receipts.

Finally, Jason said that we should go. It was getting late, and Mum and Dad would be wondering where we were. As we put the things back, Larry picked up the gold watch and slipped it into the pocket of his shorts.

We looked at him with wide eyes. 'Larry!'

'Umm! I'm telling!' said Tommy.

'Then I'm telling that you broke into Grandad's house and looked through his stuff!'

'It's not yours!'

'You can't!'

But Larry turned his back on us, ran down the hall, through the kitchen and out the back door. He pulled it shut with a slam that echoed through the rooms. The Sullivan's dog set up its barking again.

'Larry!' wailed Tommy and ran for the back door. Jase and I followed.

We headed down the path to leap the gate. Tommy got stuck. Jase and I left him there and ran after Larry's ghostly form as he scooted around the corner. Thin clouds were now moving across the sky. The moon skittered in and out of them, making shifting patches of dark and light float across the street. Larry was doing the stealth thing, shadowy tree to shadowy fence, but we knew him and we were practised. Besides, he was heavier and we were faster. We caught up to him outside our front gate. Jase jumped on his back and got his arms around Larry's neck. Larry twisted and cursed as he tried to pry Jase's arms off. Jase clung like a rodeo rider on a crazy bull. I shuffled from foot to foot and then saw my chance. I ducked in, grabbed Larry around the knees and down he came like a tree, but awkwardly, on his front with his arms pinned underneath. Still Jase hung around his neck. I added my weight and together we managed to keep him on the ground.

'Ger off!' grunted Larry.

'No! Not till you give it back,' yelled Jase.

'It's not yours!' I shouted.

Tommy was there, then. ''S not yours. 'S not yours. It's Grandad's!' he kept saying. He was crying and sniffling. He wiped his hand across his face and left a snail trail that glistened in the moonlight. He fell on his brother and beat into his shoulders, his head, anywhere that we were not sitting.

'Give it back!' he cried. Then, I think he realised that Larry's arms were caught under him because he pulled at Larry's shorts until he could reach into the pocket and take out the watch.

'Ger off, will ya!'

We let him go. He crawled away, sat, and turned to watch us. The moon hid at that moment. Larry's face went dark, but we could feel the coldness of his stare.

'Fine. You can have it then,' he said and leapt up and ran away into the night. We were left sitting on the footpath and Tommy was holding Grandad's watch. He cried, 'Larry! Wait!' tossed the watch at Jase and disappeared after his brother.

We stared at it, cold and glinting in the now-exposing moonlight.

'Bugger!' said Jase.

Dad's voice shot from the front door like the sound of a judge's gavel slamming the block, 'You kids alright?'

We sat stunned. Dad shouted again.

I called out, 'Coming,' and said to Jase, 'You gotta hide it in your room somewhere. Till we can get it back to Grandad's.'

'But Tommy's the only one who fits, 'member?'

'Oh, yeah… but did we lock the back door? Did we? Did we even shut it?'

We looked at each other wide-eyed, thinking.

'Yeah, yeah, I'm pretty sure I heard it shut.'

I nodded. 'Yeah, I think so, too.'

'Are you kids coming in? Now!' shouted Dad. 'It's late. You've got fruit-picking early tomorrow.' It was our summer job out at the Hills Orchards—Jase picked apricots and I cut them ready for drying. It paid little but it was something to do in the long holidays.

So, that was how we had Grandad's watch burning a hole in our consciences, and us scrabbling to find an opportunity to put it back.

Chapter Seven

We could hear voices coming through the kitchen window after we got back from Hills Orchards. Besides Mum's and Dad's there were voices we didn't recognise, but the man sounded like Gilligan from *Gilligan's Island*. It was Dad's favourite TV show.

'Oh, no!' I said to Jase. He was biting his lip.

Sure enough, Aunt Caroline and Uncle Bob were at the table having afternoon tea with Mum and Dad. Oma was nodding off in her comfy chair in the corner, a rug over her legs despite the heat.

Mum'd made a big effort—a fresh, crocheted tea cosy, her lace tablecloth and the Colclough china she'd been given for their wedding. She was offering fresh scones around.

'Oh, good. Emily, Jason. Look who's here!' Mum's voice was a bit higher and breathier than usual. Aunt Caroline had that effect on people, like we weren't up to scratch.

Small town hicks. Mum had no cause to feel that way. She'd come to Yarralinga to teach high school English and history (I got my smarts at English from her), she played piano in the dance band, and she was the best cook ever. But she always went quiet when Aunt Caroline was around. I was glad that wasn't often.

We stood in the doorway and said, 'Hullo.' Aunt Caroline barely flicked a smile in our direction, but Uncle Bob half rose, beaming on his flushed, wide face and said, 'Hullo, hullo,' before sinking back down again.

'Pull up a pew, kids,' said Dad. And so, we had to stay. Besides, Mum's scones were always good, and we needed to hear the conversation in case they said anything about Grandad's house. But the talk went round and round about Aunt Caroline's work, their 'lovely new, architect-designed house' with the 'absolutely stunning views over the harbour' and their 'adorable little puppy that I (Aunt Caroline) am missing sooo much'. Uncle Bob just silently ate more scones with fig jam and cream. I counted five.

Then suddenly, Aunt Caroline ran out of talking about herself and pushed up from the table. She smoothed her hands down her slim-fitting skirt (she looked about as skinny as a greyhound) and said, 'Well, I'm off to see Barb and then have a look in the house. Coming Bob?'

'No, you go. Think I'll just have a bit of shut-eye.'

I looked at Jase. There were two little creases between his eyebrows.

Aunt Caroline stood, slid on her white linen jacket, and with a 'Later,' went out the back door.

'Kids, you've got your jobs to do before tea. Bring in the

washing too, would you Emily?' said Mum, getting up from the table to stir the stew she already had cooking. We went outside to water the seedlings, feed the dog and chooks and collect the eggs. And get the washing off the line.

'What're we gunna do?'

Chapter Eight

'What if she's noticed?' My stomach was churning like a milk separator.

We were just up from the tea table and Oma had wandered off to bed, when Aunt Caroline came storming in the back door. I could easily picture her walking into the courtroom ready to annihilate the defendant.

'Who's been in the house?' she demanded, locking her lawyer stare onto Dad. I felt heat flush my face. I looked at Jase. He was concentrating on scraping his plate into the chook bucket. I followed him into the kitchen. But we could hear it all.

'No one,' replied Dad. Cool. Calm. 'I've got the keys.'

'I feel like someone's been in.'

'Well, yeah, I went in to turn things off straight after Dad went. Make sure it'd be alright. Ruthie emptied the fridge. That's it.'

'It's just that the hall runner is all askew, and Mum's

dressing table looks different, like it's been gone through. Did she give you anything before she went?'

'Nah. Like what? Why would she?' Dad's voice was rising a bit.

'You know, she might have wanted Chris or Sue or Ruth to have something to remember her by. I just feel something's missing, but I don't know what. It's been a while since I saw what Mum had.'

Dad took the bait. 'Yeah, well whose fault's that? Couldn't even come back for your own mum's funeral!'

Aunt Caroline's response was razor sharp. 'You know I was in the middle of a major suit. I couldn't leave my client high and dry, could I?' Aunt Caroline, hot-shot lawyer.

Jase and I looked at one another. We sidled out the doorway to the sound of Aunt Caroline haranguing Dad, and Uncle Bob muttering placating noises. Mum was clattering around, scraping plates and letting them drop into the sink. Jase scooted to his room and came back with his hand in his pocket. I lifted Dad's keys off the hook in the back hallway. We froze for a second when they clinked together, then slipped out the back door and skedaddled to the gate. A slightly trimmed moon was just rising. There was a breeze that smelled of summer rain, and clouds gathering on the western hills.

The fire siren rang just as we left the house. 'It's not testing night, is it?'

'Nup, it's Wednesday.'

Dad rushed past us, shoving his sleeves into his overalls as he fled out the gate and down to the fire station where men were already on board the truck and backing it out the shed.

'Great!' said Jase. 'They won't miss us. Come on.'

We headed down Sturt Street and turned into Old Coach Road. That was when we saw an orange glow coming from the house at the end—Grandad's! We ran. Smoke was billowing from the side of the house. There were people out on the footpath, yelling, as if it would stop the fire that leapt about inside the sitting room window and shot up and out the chimney like a volcano. I saw Crisps from next door and Sullivans from over the back fence. Jooles's dad, Mr Kent, was there, too, shifting uneasily from one foot to the other as he watched the devouring flames.

The fire truck bucked to a stop outside—they must've come down Railway Terrace—and the men scattered like ants to their tasks. More and more neighbours arrived to watch, hoping, too, that in the summer heat the fire wouldn't leap to their own places.

As it was, it didn't take long for the men to get it under control. We all stood around for a long time after, while they wound their hoses and cleaned down the truck, chatting through how lucky it was that Mr Kent had gone outside when he did, and that the fire had only damaged the sitting room. They'd broken the window to pour water in.

'I'm going in to have a look,' said Dad.

'I'll come,' said Jase and, looking at me, patted his pocket. I nodded.

I heard Mr Kent talking to Sergeant Forrest, his hands gesticulating wildly. It was him who'd raised the alarm. He'd gone out to turn off the hose on his tomatoes and shut the chooks up. He'd heard something in Grandad's and looked over the fence in time to see a bunch of lads hurdling the front gate. They'd hightailed it past the Railway pub. Just who or how many he couldn't say. The Sarge took off in his car. *Bit late*, I thought. I knew who they were. Well, at least one of them. *But how had Larry got inside if Tommy wasn't with them? Surely, he wasn't.*

'Em! Em!' I heard someone calling me and, peering into the backyard, I saw Jooles's head and shoulders above the back fence where the Kents and Grandad shared a few yards of corrugated iron. She must've been standing on the compost bin to get a good look.

'Is it alright?' she asked. Her face was shining white in the soft moonlight.

I climbed on the fence rails and said, 'Yeah, mostly. Thanks to your dad's quick reactions. Got no further than the sitting room.'

She relaxed, 'Good. Do you know how it started?'

Jase came out then and when he saw us, climbed up beside me.

'Done,' he said.

I nodded at him and let out a long breath of relief.

Dad called out for us to go.

'Coming,' I called.

'Nice jarmies,' said Jase to Jooles as he jumped down. She went the same shade of pink as her baby doll pjs— though it was a bit hard to tell in that light—and ducked down off the bin. 'Night,' she called as she hopped between the veggie beds in her pink bunny slippers. *That was weird. Why'd she run off so quick?*

'See you,' I called after her.

It started to rain just then. I lifted my face and felt the cool needles of fine drops on my face. *Beautiful smell. Yay!*

Sound of rain on the roof tonight. It was a consolation for having to give up my room for Aunt Caroline and Uncle Bob and sleep in the sleep-out with Jase. Oma had the third bedroom, so when people came to stay it was always me who had to move out.

But it was alright. I mean, the camp bed wasn't too uncomfortable. And the rain on the sleep-out roof was louder than in my room. And Jase was my twin. We'd both sleep better knowing that the gold watch was back where it belonged.

Chapter Nine

We heard the next day that Sergeant Forrest had caught up with the lads. Larry had taken two others into Grandad's to hang about and smoke. He'd got Tommy to open the door the night before and unlock a window. In their skylarking, one of them—they wouldn't dob on each other—had rolled some old newspaper into a cigar and lit it. It'd burned so fast that when it reached his fingers, he flicked it away. It hit the curtains and they went up like a skyrocket on Guy Fawkes.

Dad, Mum, and the aunts and uncles decided not to press charges. Except for Aunt Caroline who was livid and went for Dad with words I'd never heard before, even though Dad could swear like a trooper.

Instead, they made all the lads sign up to the CFS as punishment—'Maybe they'll learn a thing or two about the dangers of fire'—and sent them out on training exercises in the middle of stinking hot Saturdays when they would have played cricket or tennis or gone swimming. We'd see them looking deadbeat in the fire truck coming home past the waterhole.

Larry didn't last long because Aunty Chris and Uncle Ken packed him off to boarding school in Adelaide at the end of January, having been refused by Aunty Sue and Uncle Steve to have him board with them.

'That'll straighten him out, I don't think,' said Dad, sarcastically. 'He's a bad egg, that one.'

Aunty Sue and Uncle Steve came up from Adelaide and together with Aunty Chris and Uncle Ken, we spent days and days clearing Grandad's house, filling the ute with old clothing and worn linens, jars and bottles and so much junk, for trips to the dump. We'd have had a bonfire, except it was total fire ban. Years of *Advertisers* and *Women's Weeklies* got thrown onto the ute instead.

Aunt Caroline and Uncle Bob finally went home a couple of days before school went back. She took Grandma's pearls, being as she said the oldest girl and therefore entitled to them. Aunty Chris was disappointed. She said that Grandma had promised them to her. But Aunt Caroline used her lawyer techniques and Aunty Chris backed down. I saw her mouth quivering as she left the room.

Dad got the gold watch, being the oldest boy. Uncle Steve didn't care.

'Not a sentimental bone in his body,' according to Aunty Sue.

He was more interested in getting back to Adelaide and was throwing stuff on the ute before the rest had a chance to look at it. Mum and Aunty Chris saved a whole box of photos from his hasty hands.

'What in the hell are you doing, Steve! Go and… and make us a cuppa or something.'

Uncle Steve went to the pub.

When, finally, it was just Dad and Mum, Aunty Chris and Uncle Ken, we spent a couple of days setting up for a clearing sale. Dad posted house-for-sale notices around town and outside Carey's Grocery—the shop that Dad and Mum joint-owned with Aunty Chris and Uncle Ken.

SALE DAY WAS a day of burning heat. 'Boiling in the water bag, I reckon,' said Dad as he lifted his hat and wiped his sweating face and neck.

Mum, my aunts and I stood under the scant shade of the pepper tree and watched crowds of people from all over, even as far away as Kimba, inspecting Grandad and Grandma's things and sometimes exclaiming over what they'd found. They only went silent when the auctioneer started up his, 'Hup, what'm I bid, what'm I bid…' and 'Sold!' Then, sometimes, people clapped. Or moaned if they failed to win the bid. It felt weird to see things that had been in Grandad's house for years being taken away by other people. Even stuff that I thought was worthless, like some of Grandad's rusty tools and boxes of assorted kitchen bits. The stuff you throw in the bottom drawer and forget what it was for. Or that it's there.

Jooles came with her dad. He bought some garden equipment and a chaff cutter so he could chop up lucerne for his chooks. He looked chuffed to have won the bids on them.

'These'll be put to good use, Emily,' he said kindly. I reckon he could see I was finding it all a bit hard.

So did Jooles. 'Come on, Em. Let's get outta here. You don't have to stay, do you?'

So, I told Mum we were going, and we jumped the back fence into Jooles's place. I felt heavy in my chest. Like a block of ice sat there.

'You alright?' asked Jooles. 'You miss your grandparents, eh?'

I started to cry then, partly because what she said was true and partly because she said it. Jooles was a good friend.

PART III
JOOLES

Chapter Ten

1st February 1970

Em's oma lived with them. She was her great-grandma really. Her name was Mrs Scholz, and she and Mr Scholz had lived in Adelaide long before World War I. But because he was a German businessman, when the war began he was sent to the Torrens Island Internment Camp just in case he was a spy. Em told me once about how horrible it was and how he died there before the war finished. Mrs Scholz'd had a really tough life providing for their four children, including Em's grandma.

Oma would sit in a wicker chair on their front veranda for most of the day, watching the world go by and poking her stick at the dog when it lay down on her feet. She didn't speak much English and I don't think she understood much either. She was a tiny little lady, all bent up and wizened, with floppy skin hanging from her forearms and neck. I think she'd known a lot of pain and lack in her early life, maybe not got much good food and so didn't grow much.

Sometimes, when I went to their place, Em would be bashing away at her piano practice—she did it because her mum wanted her to, not because she enjoyed it at all. (Her mum was a good pianist and played in the dance band.) Then, instead of going inside, I'd sit down near Mrs Scholz.

'Tag,' she said this day, even though she hadn't touched me. I thought she was making a joke, so I touched her arm quickly and said, 'Tag.' Her eyes twinkled.

We sat companionably silent for a while as Em's faltering chords tumbled through the sitting-room window. When the piano lid banged shut and I got up to go inside, Mrs Scholz said, 'Juice.' I turned back to her and said, 'Oh, sure.'

Em was still shuffling around with her music books, so I went to the kitchen and got a glass of juice for Mrs Scholz. Em met me in the hallway on my way back.

'For your oma,' I said.

'Oh, thanks, but she doesn't like juice.'

'She said she wanted some though.'

'Really?'

We went outside together, and I put the juice on the table next to Mrs Scholz. She looked strangely at me and then at Em who just shrugged her shoulders and said, 'Come on, Jooles, let's go. Bye, Oma.'

'Juice,' said Mrs Scholz.

'See,' I said. 'Juice. She said it again.'

Em laughed. 'Not juice. Tschüss! She's saying "bye". Tschüss, Oma.'

'Bye,' called Mrs Scholz with a flick of her skinny hand. She giggled like a little girl.

I went red and then called, 'Tschüss, Mrs Scholz,' as we wheeled our bikes down the path. 'Well, that was awkward.'

'Don't worry about it. You made her laugh. And she doesn't do that much.'

We rode off down to Old Coach Road, past the shops and the war memorial, to head out to the waterhole. It was the Saturday before school went back. Lots of the townies were there making the most of the last day of freedom, clowning around on the rope swing and falling into the cool water, or lying on towels under the gums, chatting in the afternoon heat. There was a group of matric kids lazing under the furthest gum, keeping well away from us 'little kids'. They'd be leaving for town in a couple of weeks to uni and work. We'd rarely see them anymore. Patrick, Sean and Conal were yabbying down at the very far end where the creek narrowed. Not sure they were having much luck because they were throwing out the lamb shank and hauling it in a bit too fast.

Gracie Burton and Liz White called to us to join them on the bank, so we spread our towels next to theirs. 'You coming in?' Em asked as she stripped to her bathers.

'Yeah,' said Liz.

But Gracie said, 'Think I'll stay in the shade till the sun goes down a bit.' She'd got burnt so badly in Grade Seven that she was in hospital for a week while the blisters went down. She had a gorgeous pair of olive-green bathers that suited her red hair.

Michael Boston came up then and shook his wet hair

over her. 'Cool?' he asked, and she laughed. He parked himself down next to her, so we left and ran for the water, joining the others skylarking, splashing and riding on each other's shoulders to see who could push the other off.

I spotted Candy Murphy and her friend, Skye, lounging on the trunk of the gum that had fallen across the creek. They were wearing crocheted bikinis (I recognised the pattern from the *Women's Weekly* lift-out) and acting like they were sunbathing on the Riviera. It must have worked because the boys were getting stupid with their pranks off the swing rope. Peter May tried a backflip but didn't get enough height. He hit the water with the loudest smack and disappeared. Everyone held their breath until he came up, gulping. He turned without looking toward the girls on the tree trunk and swam for the bank where he just hung in the reeds like a stunned mullet. Candy and Skye snickered even after other kids gave them the stare. Michael went to see if Peter was alright and hauled him out. His back was red where he'd hit the water and he sort of crouched along to fall in a heap on his towel. Poor kid.

'Where's Jase?' asked Michael when we went back to our towels.

'Tennis,' said Em.

'Man, hot for playing tennis. Home or away?'

'Here. Should be finished soon. Said he'd come for a swim after.'

'Great.'

It was so hot, even in the shade. Oven hot. The heat bounced back off the ground and dried out our eyes and nostrils. We were dry in no time, so back in the water we went. We lost count of how many times we swam, then lay on our towels and then swam again. Then finally, the sun fell below the gums and the waterhole was in shadow. 'No excuses now,' said Michael as he pulled Gracie to her feet and down to the water.

Candy and Skye had slithered away. *Good riddance!*

Jase and Tom Lawson arrived in their tennis whites. They dropped their bikes, stripped to the waist and ran for the rope, swinging out to fall into the water. 'Yahoo!' yelled Tom as he came up.

Finally, as we lay around, Liz said, 'So, school Monday,' and everybody groaned.

'Sorry,' she said. 'But you know…' She shrugged, pulled her ponytail over her shoulder and wrung it out.

'Yeah, just didn't really want to think about it yet.'

There was silence for a bit. Then Tom said, 'Wonder if Mr Mullins is back this year?'

'I heard he was.' Mr Mullins was a favourite teacher, strict but fair, young and good-looking. We wondered if Miss O'Connell would still be there. They might finally start going out. We talked about other teachers we hoped would be back and who we hoped had left, what classes we liked and what ones we hated.

Then Tom changed the subject. 'Didja hear about old Mrs Hillman? The cat lady.'

'Yeah, my brother found her,' said Liz. 'Well, he didn't actually see her, but he knew something was wrong 'cos the box of groceries was still on the veranda from the week before, and he could hear cats yowling.'

'She was a weird old bird.'

'I don't remember ever seeing her.'

'No, don't think she ever went out. So how do you know she was weird? What sorta weird?'

'My dad said she couldn't remember people. Even forgot who her sister was. Even herself. And the house stank of cats.'

'Yeah, forty!'

'I heard twenty-three.'

'Whatever. It was still too many.'

We were quiet, thinking. Michael said, 'Does that make her weird though? I mean, isn't that just sad?'

We mumbled agreement. Awkwardly. Like we'd been caught telling fibs.

Tom jumped in again. 'So, I heard that Larry's been sent to boarding school.'

And we latched onto the new topic like a lifeline.

Chapter Eleven

We were changing for sport. I wished we could change in the toilet cubicles, but we had to change in the same room as all the other girls. Em and I made our way into a corner as far away from the others as we could.

'Didja see Justin?' breathed Candy salaciously. She sounded like a six-year-old in a lolly shop salivating over bobby dazzlers and fizzy pops, chocolate buttons and milk bottles. Her friends surrounded her, eyes lit, nodding so their high ponies bounced about their necks.

'Ooo, he's so yummy!'

'His arms! Muscles bigger than my dad's.'

'Yeah! Remember how skinny he used to be?'

I thought I could see drool leaking from the side of Skye's mouth.

Em got caught. 'Why's that?' she asked.

Candy scoffed. 'Didn't you notice?' She drew back her shoulders so her well-filled, lacy B-cups pushed forward. She flicked her hair and lifted her chin to look down on Em with that I'm-a-grown-woman-and-you're-still-a-little-girl look. Her friends giggled and eyed Candy out the corner of their eyes, nodding in knowing agreement.

Em's eyes fell on those rounded boobs. It was a bit hard not to look, with them being so close to her face. She bit her lip, wondering what to reply, I think, but then turned to the wall to hide her flat chest and the creep of red that was racing up her neck toward her face.

Candy gave a leering laugh which became a snort and went back to salivating with her followers over the physical virtues of Justin Waters.

I nudged my shoulder against Em's in a show of solidarity. I felt her embarrassment like my own. I changed next to her, aware of Mum's words as she'd paid for my training bra in the last holidays, 'You're just a late-bloomer, Julie, that's all,' as if that was supposed to make me feel better. I could feel the stares of the girls on us. We dressed fast, then scooted out the door to join the boys, who were always first to PE.

Em seemed to shake the episode off and launched herself into the game—basketball, mixed teams. Sport was her absolute favourite, and she was fantastic at everything. She always got age champion at inter-school sports, and in Grades Six *and* Seven, she was chosen to go to the SAPSASA carnival in Adelaide to play women's basketball.

So, she just played like it was the best part of the day which, for her, I guess it was.

Every now and then, I side-eyed Justin Waters. Yep, he

had changed over the holidays—in a sort of muscly way—and when I tried to tackle the ball off him, I saw a soft, pale fuzz on his top lip. I could smell him too—not the hot, acrid smell of sweat that hung around most of the other boys and made me gasp, but a faint smell of Brut.

CANDY WAS SUPERCILIOUS. I'd liked that word ever since Gramma read me *King John's Christmas* by A.A. Milne. Supercilious. I loved the way it rolled around my mouth and ended with an 's' that I could hiss when I thought about Candy Murphy and her super-silly, snooty, stuck-up ways. How she looked down her nose at everyone.

We went to the drive-in once to see *Mary Poppins*. I memorised the Supercalifragilistic song and sang it under my breath when I saw Candy, but then I found it meant 'something wonderful'. Erg! Nope! Supercilioussss was definitely the right word.

She started writing her name in full with a little heart over the 'i' instead of the dot—Candice. Sometimes, she just wrote Candi. Lorrie copied, but Skye had trouble because Skie looked really silly.

Candy was out there, always flirting with the boys, winding her hair around her fingers while giggling at their stupid jokes—even ones that made fun of her—pretending to stumble over their feet so she could catch her balance by grabbing them, or last winter, dancing around so that her tunic lifted to show her black-with-red-frills witches' britches. Mine were standard and practical—navy like our tunic, no frills, covering my freezing thighs above my stockings. Like Mum said, 'Why frills when no one's going to see them anyway?' Yeah, well…

I was so glad when Drake's Drapery *finally* got pantyhose and I could ditch the suspenders and the witches' britches for good.

Chapter Twelve

Easter 1970

Sure enough, Larry hated boarding school, especially its food. Em's Uncle Ken and Aunty Chris got a package from him that made the postie gag. Aunty Chris nearly put it straight in the bin, but Uncle Ken held his nose and snipped the tape. Inside the wrappings was a box with a furry green chop on a mess of mouldy mash and limp beans. It stank like the abattoirs. There was a note: 'This is the crap they feed us here. I wanna come home.'

They talked to Em's Uncle Steve and Aunty Sue in Adelaide again. Their kids had moved out, so they said, well, alright... they'd have Larry with them. Just for a trial. See how it goes.

Some people from Adelaide bought Em's Grandad's place. They moved in over the Easter weekend. I was out in the backyard with Dad, making the most of the glorious autumn weather, when we heard their car pull into the driveway and Sullivan's dog start barking up and down the adjoining fence. Mr Sullivan next door, who was also making the most of the sunshine to chop some firewood for winter, cut crook at his dog, 'Shudup! Si'down!'

The dog yelped, whined and went quiet. We heard car doors shut, people talking and going into the house.

'Must be the new folks arrived,' said Dad. 'Let's get a basket ready to welcome 'em.'

We picked a few last tomatoes, still a bit green, and some apples and pears. Mum added a few bottles of her tomato sauce. Then Dad, Mum with Brigid, and I went around to meet the new people.

They were at their car when we walked in the front gate. The woman glanced up and straight away turned her back and headed for the house. The man looked up and stepped forward with his hand out to shake Dad's hand.

'Hullo,' said Dad. 'Barry Kent. We live over the back.' He pointed down the side of the house to where our faded red roof showed above the fence and Dad's tomato trellis. 'So, I guess you're our new neighbours.'

Mum said, 'We wanted to come around and say welcome to Yarralinga.'

The man's wide smile showed his teeth through his gingery beard. His blond hair hung right to his shoulders. He was lanky and wore a loose shirt over his jeans and a pair of thongs.

'Hullo,' he said. 'Really good of you. Hans Larsen.' He shook Dad's hand.

Dad said, 'My wife, Fiona, and this is Julie and little Brigid. Our eldest and youngest.'

'Lovely to meet you,' Hans replied. 'Lily's just doing some unpacking. I'd invite you in, but we really only just got here.'

'No, no, of course. We didn't expect you to,' said Mum. 'Here. These are a few things from our garden to help you get started.'

Hans took the basket and thanked Mum and Dad with another bright smile. 'Wow! Thank you!'

Dad looked at the boarded-up sitting-room window. The frame was blackened from the fire. 'Got your work cut out for you, I reckon. I can give you a hand if you want, to fix up the damage to the room.'

'Thanks. I appreciate the offer, but I'll get it done sometime. We don't really need the room straight away.'

'Well, Hans,' said Mum as she prodded Dad. 'We'll let you get back to moving in. Just give us a hoy if we can help with anything. You know, where things are—doctor, chemist, firewood, all that sort of thing.'

As we walked home, Mum said, 'Did you see the girl almost run inside when she saw us? Must be really shy.'

I WAS INTRIGUED by the new couple. I was over at Em's place one Saturday when Em asked her dad if he knew anything about them. She thought they might have come into the shop and her dad would have served them.

He said, 'Nah, not much. Bloody hippy. Looks like a Neanderthal. Needs to clean himself up a bit!'

Em's mum shot back, 'Brian! That's a dreadful thing to say!'

I'd never heard her raise her voice at him before. Jase was a bit taken aback too. I could see from the way he looked at his dad.

'Well,' said Mr Price, 'what does he do, anyway? Doesn't work anywhere. Prob'ly on the dole.' Most towns-people were of the opinion that being on the dole was a sin greater than robbing the church offertory bag.

Em's mum said, 'Leave it, Brian. Don't talk mean of people. They paid for the house, you got the money, so just leave it be.'

'Wow,' said Em later. 'Never heard Mum stick up for people like that before.'

I SPIED on the Larsens through the gaps in our back fence. Lily was sitting on the veranda, spinning. She wore a long, floaty dress with her thick, wavy, honey-blonde hair loose over her right shoulder. I felt a pang of envy—my hair was mousy brown according to Granny Murphy. Lily was looking down and her hair was a golden screen down her face. She was concentrating on pulling the wool and letting the wheel take it in. Effortlessly. Her foot treadled up and down in a soothing rhythm. I was mesmerised.

Hans appeared from the shed with a garden fork in his hand. He sort of loped along, all gangly like the baby giraffe I saw in the zoo once. He paused next to Lily and said something to her. As she lifted her head, her hair fell back. I sucked in a breath. The right side of her face was a mess—the skin stretched, scarred and red. Her right eye was partly hidden by skin pulled across it. Ugly. But the other side of her face was really pretty.

Hans leaned down and kissed her lips. She smiled as she gazed up at him. A warm feeling filled me. This was good. They were in love. It was as if I was looking at a young Mum and Dad. Like I was looking into my future. Maybe. Hopefully.

'What're you doing there, Jooles?'

Dad's voice gave me such a fright that I jumped. I know I turned red—I could feel it flood my face.

'Not good to spy on other people, girlie. Might see something you can't unsee.'

I swallowed and nodded.

Then Dad smiled. He dropped his voice. 'So, what'd you see that made you grin like a Cheshire cat?'

I said softly, 'Lily. Did you know about her face?'

We kept our voices low and moved to the other end of the garden bed near the chook house so they couldn't hear.

'Ah, yes, I know. Pretty sad, eh? But that wouldn't make you grin.'

'Oh, that. I saw him kiss her. Even with her face like that.'

Dad nodded and smiled. 'Yep, pretty special, eh? Yep. That'd make you smile.'

'But why's her face like that, Dad?'

'Not sure, but I think she was in a fire. Maybe Hans'll tell us when we get to know them a bit more. Don't think she goes out much. I guess she feels embarrassed having people stare at her. Must get pretty lonely, though.'

SURE ENOUGH, it was Hans who did their shopping and banking. It made the gossips talk and make up all sorts of stories about Lily. Mrs Hawkins said to Mrs Vincent, 'Heard her first husband locked her and the kids in the car and set it alight. She was the only one who survived.'

'Really?' said Mrs Vincent. 'Well, *I* heard that she was smoking in bed and went to sleep and lit the house on fire. She got out, but her kids didn't.'

Mr Sullivan told Em's dad that he could hear 'that hippy guy' in his shed making something out of wood or sometimes scratching and chipping away at stone. And welding, too.

'Yeah,' said Em's dad. 'I heard he's an artist or something.' He said it like it was a disease or akin to rummaging in the rubbish dump for a living.

'Waster!' said Mr Sullivan.

And on and on the rumours went. Hurtful, destructive slurs. But I was still intrigued—I had so many unanswered questions. Hans and Lily were different from most people in our town, and from my spying through the fence, I couldn't see truth in what people said.

Chapter Thirteen

Term 2, Intermediate

When I was little, my older cousin Rachel, who lived in Adelaide, used to send me a parcel of hand-me-down clothes at the end of every summer and again at the end of winter. I looked forward to getting them. They were things that weren't available in Drake's Drapery or Bloomingdale's or the op shop, which were the only clothes shops in Yarralinga. I loved the feel of them, the way they smelled of Rachel's perfume or Aunty Deidre's washing powder, the way they made me dream that there was a far bigger world than what I knew. I'd try them on in front of the cheval mirror in Mum and Dad's room so I could see the full length of me, not just the top bit that my own mirror showed.

I twirled around and tried to mimic Rachel's swaying-hipped walk. I giggled behind my hand like Rachel did at the Christmas dinner table when her dad told an off-colour joke. I puffed out my still-flat chest to try to fill the bodice like Rachel's boobs did. I tried to *be* Rachel.

I had a crush on Justin Waters. He was in the year ahead and always had the girls fluttering when he walked past. He was athletic and muscular when most of the boys in my class were still pretty weedy. He was always age champion on sports days. He had this cute-looking shock of blond hair that fell across his forehead into one eye so that he often had to push it back. His eyes were blue. After the mid-year dinner dance, the grapevine whispered of him and Skye Skinner doing it out behind the gardener's shed. She did nothing to dispel the rumours. In fact, she fuelled them by keeping her mouth closed, her chin high and wearing this sort of smug look on her face as if we were just a bunch of kids (which we were) and she an adult now. I did think it was a bit strange though—that night had been a hard frost. Behind the gardener's shed? Really?

Justin went out with most of the girls in our year and his, and even with some who had left school to work in shops or on their parents' farms. He made blatant, crude hand gestures to the newest girlfriend as the weekend bell rang and we herded through the school gates. His mates sniggered and the girls usually had the grace to colour and duck their heads. Then on Mondays, he gloated about his weekend conquests to his mates. None of the girls survived more than a couple of dates before he moved on to the next. But it seemed there was some sort of competition among them to see who could snare him the longest. They still simpered when he went by, almost shouting, 'Choose me!'

But not Em. 'Idiot!' she'd mutter. I thought she might go for him, being athletic and loving her sports and all. But no,

I reckon she had him sussed and valued herself more than
most of the girls that fell for him. I never let on to her that I
had a crush on him.

By the time he noticed me toward the end of term two,
Justin Waters had a reputation as long as a stinking-hot
summer night and I wasn't even sure that I wanted
him to notice me anymore. I remembered Rachel's
hand-me-downs and I knew I had a choice. If I went
out with him, it'd be as if I was putting on Rachel's
coat or shirt or dress, and acting out being her. As if I
was trying to be someone else. Justin Waters was really
nothing more than a second-hand shirt—stained and
used.

When I said this to Em, she said, 'Maybe he's just worn
in, you know, like when you wear jeans a few times and
they get soft and saggy in the bum.' We fell about laughing
at that.

Then and there I decided that I'd take the other choice.
I'd gone right off him. I'd rather a new pair of jeans that I
could make soft and saggy and only mine.

'Hey, Jooles,' Justin said. He swaggered up to me and Em
as we waited for Mr Mullins to open the science lab. He
leant his arm against the door frame above my head so that
I had to look up at him. I caught a strong whiff of stale
ciggie that made me cough.

'I's wondrin' if you wanna go out this weekend? Maybe the drive-in?'

I slipped out from under his arm to the other side of the door and tried to suppress a laugh by turning it into another cough. Em didn't succeed so well. Her loud laugh turned to a snort. She had the best laugh. I always wondered how such a small person could produce such volume. Maybe all her sports gave her big lung capacity. Anyway, Justin stepped back and stared at her then me. He looked baffled. Probably no other girl had reacted that way to his invitation.

'No thanks,' I said.

'Yeah? No? C'mon. I can pick you up. Dad said I can have the car Sat'dee night.'

Em had controlled herself by this time. 'She said no, you moron. Leave off!'

'Aww, c'mon. It's just the drive-in.'

'Yeah, right!' Em moved up and poked him in the chest. 'Rack off, Justin. Just the drive-in, my fat uncle!'

Man, she was good! Justin went this pretty shade of pink and slunk off backwards around the corner of the science lab just as the bell rang and Mr Mullins opened the door. We went inside giggling, with me hugging her around the shoulders in gratitude.

Trouble is, later that day when we were at the bike racks with Jase, unlocking our bikes to ride home, other kids were looking at us weirdly, pointing and sniggering. We rode off down Wattle Street and stopped where Em and Jase turned left into Murray, and I turned right.

'What was that all about?' I asked Jase.

'Huh, you don't wanna know.'

'Yes, we do,' said Em.

Jase shrugged. 'Justin Waters is saying you don't go for guys. Only girls.'

'What?' we shouted together.

'Yeah, 'cos you turned him down.'

'Hah, total MORON!' yelled Em. 'He'd better watch out.' She turned back toward the school as if expecting Justin to still be there so she could poison him with her stare. But he'd left on the bus.

Jase shrugged. 'Leave it be, Em. He's not worth it.'

'See ya',' I mumbled and rode off, feeling sick in my stomach. I hated that people thought wrong of me.

<hr>

THE NEXT DAY WAS WORSE. There was a bunch of kids who loved nothing more than being catty and bitchy. They latched onto Justin's lies like Schneider's dog onto sheep. Of course, Candy was right in there, hanging around Justin and his mates, sniggering, pointing at us and making crude remarks that only we could hear, not the teachers.

It became too hard to hang out together so, by some unspoken agreement, Em and I kept apart at school, sat on opposite sides of the classrooms and kept distance between us when we were riding home.

Sometimes, I'd go around to hers on the weekend, but it was never the same. The lies niggled away in my mind, and I began to wonder if there was any truth in them, at least from Em's side. I thought about the rumours that went around town about Hans and Lily. Was there any truth in them?

I started hanging around with Liz, Gracie and Rosie. They accepted me into their group as if I'd been there always.

I felt bad for Em though, when I saw her by herself, out running around the track at lunchtimes. I missed her. A hollowness in my chest.

PART IV
EMILY

Chapter Fourteen

Robby Smith's uncle gave him a Polaroid camera. He took weird photos of his friends from strange angles (up under the chin, down the face from above) or closeups (eyes, nostrils, ears) and stuck them up around school. We'd be walking to another class and there'd be a photo of Justin with his tongue touching his nose pasted to the Art room door. Or on the basketball pole, one of a kid's hand, so outstretched toward the camera it looked alien-big.

He snuck up on people too and took photos without them knowing.

I was in the library one Friday lunchtime, partly to research a history assignment, but mostly because it was lonely at lunch without Jooles to hang around with. I was standing by the shelf with a book open, trying to decide if it was what I needed, when Candy appeared and stood beside me. Close. Too close. I moved a step sideways. She did the same. Still too close. I turned toward her.

'You want this book?' I asked. Even though I knew she didn't do history.

She smirked and leaned toward me just as I heard a sound in the bookshelf. I turned my head to look. Candy's mouth hit my cheek in a wet kiss. I heard a click. Robby's camera lens was staring back at me. If I hadn't turned my head right then, her lips would have landed on mine.

Next day, there was a crowd of snickering first years around the bubblers. I heard someone say, 'Girls kissing! Yuck!' A photo was stuck to the wall above them—Candy Murphy planting a kiss on my cheek, my eyes staring wide at the camera. I pushed in, pulled it down and ground it under my heel until it was so filthy no one could recognise it.

'Uh-mmm, telling! Keep 'straya bewdiful!' one of the idiots yelled at me.

I took off for the bike rack with my eyes stinging.

***

I COULDN'T STAY at school. I rode out past the dam and kept riding until the tears so blinded my eyes I had to stop. I dropped my bike on the ground and flopped beside it. But the grass was wet from last night's rain—my back was soaked straight away. I got up and threw stones at a stobie pole. I yelled at the galahs sitting on the phone lines, but they just raised their crests at me and screeched. I stomped around until I finally calmed down and started to shiver because of my wet back. Then, I picked up my bike and rode home.

Oma was on the front veranda already, even though it

was still in the morning shade. At least she had her mohair rug over her knees. She nodded to me as I slunk past.

I could hear the wireless in the kitchen and Mum's Mixmaster whirring. I slid into my room and closed the door as quietly as I could.

And stayed there until I heard Jase prop his bike against the shed wall and come inside. He tapped on my door, came in and sat on the bed next to me.

'Hey, Em. Sorry about the picture.'

'Yeah. It's not your fault.'

'Nah, but you know… sorry it happened. Robby's an idiot. Mr Thomas found out and the camera got confiscated. He's banned cameras from school.'

'Good.' I nodded. 'And Robby and Candy?'

'Yeah, spent the morning with Mr Thomas. Saw their mums go in, too. Reckon Justin put 'em up to it.'

'Of course, he did.'

I told Jase then about the possibility of a sports scholarship in Adelaide that Mr Kipling had told me about.

He was quiet for a bit. Then he said, 'You want to go?'

'I think so. Yeah, I do.'

'It's not just to get away from this rotten stuff, is it?'

I shrugged. 'I guess. A bit. But you know I really want to do sport for a job. Mr Kipling says this'd be a good way to get into it.'

He nodded.

I know we're not identical of course, but you can tell we're twins. When he looked at me, I felt like I was seeing myself.

'I'd miss you, Em,' he said.

Tears welled up then. It was the one reason I'd stay.

Chapter Fifteen

I couldn't talk to Mum. I don't really know why. I know she loved me, but it was like there was a wall between us. I think there was a wall around Mum, really, like she was trying to keep herself inside and safe. I tried to talk to her about stuff—you know, girls' stuff—but she was embarrassed or nervous and cut me off before I got out what I wanted to say or ask.

She never went out much or had many friends. Jooles's mum was the closest friend she had and that was only when Mrs Kent came by. Mum never dropped over to their place.

She grew up in Kapunda, went to teachers' college in Adelaide, taught in the city for a while and then moved to Yarralinga High. She was already pretty old by then—at least twenty-eight. But Dad fell for her, and they got married. Oma came to live with them. Soon after, Jase and I came along.

I sat next to Mum while she mended one of Dad's shirts, fiddling with the pins on her pincushion, trying to find the right way to ask her about the sports scholarship. Mum was silent, focusing on her needle piercing the fabric. She didn't even try to fill the silence with words. Did she even know I was there? The silence was as uncomfortable as me. Only words could settle it. That or get up and leave.

I went out and sat next to Oma on the front veranda.

She was soaking up the late-afternoon winter sun like a lizard on a rock, eyes half-closed and a dreamy look on her face. Oma doesn't understand much English and I don't have the right German words, so it's like Mr Kent talking to his tomatoes—you don't expect an answer. I embarrassed him once, coming around the corner of the tank stand thinking Jooles was out the back with her dad. But only Mr Kent was there kneeling by his Grosse Lisse and crooning, 'What a beauty you are.' He went the colour of the ripe tomato in his hand when he noticed me. I didn't ask if the plant had thanked him for the compliment. Jase would have, but I'm not quite that cheeky.

Anyway, I sat down next to Oma, and she smiled at me. I began to rattle on about the scholarship: should I apply or not, and what would it be like to leave home and my friends, and Jase most of all. It'd be good to get away from Justin's horrible rumours. But I'd really miss Jooles. I'd love to play sport for a job one day, maybe even get to the Olympics. I bounced the pros and cons around as if I was deciding which person I was going to throw the basketball to.

Then I just ran out of steam. I sighed and looked out

over the veranda railing at a couple of magpies warbling on the fence.

Oma patted my hand. She nodded and smiled. 'Nice day.'

'Yeah. Thanks, Oma,' I said. I pulled on my sandshoes and went for a run.

I GOT into the pounding rhythm of my feet, the familiar feel of strength in my legs, the momentum rather than feelings of indecision. *Interschool sports, interschool sports, gunna beat that girl, gunna beat that girl, leave her in the dust…*

My head was clearing with the cold on my face, so cold my eyes were watering. Heavy, grey clouds rolled over. I was part way around Crystal Lake track when icy rain fell and, I don't know why, but I started to cry. *Damn Justin Waters! Damn Candy Murphy! It's not fair…* And my mind forgot about playing sport and filled with hate and pain and unfairness and imaginings of revenge. I wanted to be as far away from them and their friends as possible. My nose was running as fast as me, making it harder and harder to breathe. I swiped at my eyes but still couldn't see, so I stopped and doubled over with my hands on my knees, panting and sniffling and feeling like rubbish.

I'll show 'em. I'll be the best. I'll make it to the Olympics! I blew my nose on my t-shirt and jogged home.

Next morning, I studied myself in the mirror, twisting from right to left. I pinched my waist, groaned, and turned to pull on my uniform. On my way out the gate, I threw the fritz and sauce sandwich Mum had made for my lunch to the dog. He wolfed it down and thumped his tail on the ground in approval.

PART V
JOOLES

Chapter Sixteen

Term 3, Intermediate

We were in English. Mrs Newman was introducing an assignment where we had to team up with two others and prepare a debate. I hated debating. I looked across at Em. Usually, before, we would've teamed up, and probably with Jase if we had to have mixed teams. But she was looking away, avoiding me. Yeah, I got it.

Mrs Newman said, 'I'll give out topics after you find your groups. No fussing, or I'll put you in groups myself. Go!'

I stood slowly, wondering what to do. Suddenly, Gracie and Lizzy were there.

'Wanna join us?'

'Yeah, join us?'

I breathed out, relieved. 'Yes, thanks!'

I glanced across to see Em with Rosie and Suzy and felt

glad for her. Suzy was a brain. If you got to be in her group, you'd be sure to get good marks.

Our topic was 'Sticks and stones will break your bones, but names will never hurt you.' It was good we were debating the negative—I knew that names could stab and twist like a knife. Even worse than sticks and stones. At least I'd have something to say that I believed in.

On the day, I stumbled through my points, my mouth as dry as the bottom of a cocky's cage, all the while aware of Candy and Lorrie whispering behind their hands. Mrs Newman had no idea as she made notes in her book.

But Lizzy did a great job of wrapping up our argument, even though we didn't win. Suzy's group did. Of course. I was glad for Em.

That lunchtime, Gracie and Lizzy invited me to their church—well, to Girls Group that the minister's wife ran. They'd been going for a while, they said, and it was a lot of fun. Mrs Friend made them laugh as well as think about all sorts of stuff, like how God wants us to live. Sometimes, she played a guitar for them to sing God songs. She had a beautiful voice.

I thought, *A girls-only group? That'd be fuel for the rumours for sure.*

I said, 'Thanks, but Mum and Dad really need me at home to help with the kids on Friday nights.'

They pestered me a bit, but then gave up and wandered away to join Rosie, leaving me to eat lunch by myself. I opened my book to the bookmarked page and escaped.

⎯⎯⎯⎯⎯

I GOT HOME one afternoon to find Mrs Friend having a cuppa with Mum. They had their backs to the kitchen sink. I smiled inside knowing that Mum had placed Mrs Friend on that side of the table so she wouldn't be looking at the messy kitchen bench.

'Hi, sweetheart,' called Mum. 'Join us.'

Mum poured me a cup of tea and I sat across from them. I could hear the twins and Maria and Kathleen outside chasing around the lawn. I could see—out the kitchen window behind Mum—the top of the Hills hoist going around and around and wondered if Mum knew the kids had tied a rope to it and were using it like a merry-go-round.

'Hi,' said Mrs Friend. 'Did you have a good day?'

'Yes, thanks.'

'Your mum says you're in Intermediate.'

I mumbled a yes, my lips on the teacup, and watched her over the rim. I guessed she was a bit older than Mum. She was wearing pale-blue eyeshadow, mascara and pink lippy, and her hair was swept up softly in a French twist with strands hanging down in front of her ears. She wore a paisley-patterned shirt in pinks and purples. She looked so different from the last minister's wife. Modern. Shiny. Fresh. She wouldn't have been out of place on the front of a *New Idea*.

'I was just telling your mum about a little friendship group I have going at my place on Friday nights. Grace, Elizabeth and Rosemary have been coming. Suzanne some-times comes.'

I did a double take. *Who are Grace, Elizabeth and Rose-*

mary? Suzanne? Then I twigged that she meant Gracie, Liz and Rosie and Suzy.

She went on. 'I wondered if you might like to come along, Julie?'

I have to help Mum. 'Maybe. They told me they go and what you do.'

'Well, have a think about it. We would love to welcome you in. And if you can come up with a more interesting name than Girls Group, that'd be wonderful. I'm not very imaginative there, I'm afraid.' She smiled widely.

Later, Mum told me I should go.

'But what about helping with the kids and everything. You need me.'

'Oh Julie, Dad and I can manage. It's important you have time with girlfriends outside of school.' She could see I wasn't keen. 'Is there another reason you don't want to go?'

I sighed. 'It's a girls-only group, Mum. You know what some of the kids at school say about me and Em. This'd only make it worse.'

She pulled me in for a hug and kissed my forehead. 'Then, my love, you have to be bigger than them. Don't play their game. You know who you are, so be that.'

Did I? Did I know who I was?

Chapter Seventeen

Birthdays were a bit hit-and-miss in our house. Mostly miss. Mum and Dad did what they could but, with eleven of us in the family, it seemed it was always a birthday. Sometimes, Dad killed a chook for Mum to pluck and clean, but if he did that for everyone, it'd mean he wouldn't have any layers left. So, usually, we only had chook for Christmas—the old ones that didn't lay anymore.

Mum sometimes forgot our birthdays, which maybe was fine because she usually forgot her own. The boys didn't really care. But Maria and Kathleen and I did. I wanted to feel special like Em did on hers, when her mum tried different recipes for tea, and we went over to celebrate her. And Jase.

When Maria started to learn about calendars, she kept one from the Yarralinga Farm Services and Garage—they gave them out to valued customers and workers every Christmas. She hung it from the blind cord in our bedroom and marked each day off when she climbed into bed. She had all our birthdays marked on it and would excitedly announce, 'It's *your* birthday tomorrow, James and Aiden!' or whoever's it happened to be. And James and Aiden would shout, 'Yay!' but not really know what that meant because when tomorrow came there wasn't much to be excited about. Just another day, really. Maybe a bit more to eat for tea, and a sponge cake with candles courtesy of Gramma Kent.

So, when my birthday came around on September fourth, and Maria announced that it was 'Jooles's birthday tomorrow, everyone! She'll be fifteen', I said, 'Yay!' and didn't expect anything different at all.

'Happy birthday, my love,' said Mum as I came out for breakfast. She'd remembered! Maria and Kathleen were close behind, dressed for school with hair already done. Mum kissed my cheek and went back to serving up the scrambled eggs. There was a brown-paper parcel sitting at my spot at the table. Sean and Conal were arguing over whose turn it was for the toy in the cornflakes packet.

'Quit the racket,' said Dad, 'or I'll have it.' They quietened.

'Happy birthday, girlie,' said Dad. 'Oi, Patrick, that's enough sauce!'

As I sat down, Kathleen cried, 'Open it, Jooles, open it!' She was more excited than me. I thought I knew what it would be. And I was right. Some hairbands and a beanie that Mum had bought from the Guild trading table.

'Put it on,' said Maria and she sighed because it was her favourite colour—pink.

'No hats at the table,' parroted Conal.

I stuck my tongue out at him and pulled the beanie on, even though I'd already done my hair for school.

'Looks good,' said Mum as she placed my breakfast in front of me.

'Thanks, Mum, Dad.'

School was much the same. Not many people knew it was my birthday. Of course, Em did and gave me a card that she'd made and a cake of home-made lavender soap that I think her Mum had bought from the good old Guild trading table. And at recess, Jase called, 'Hey, happy birthday, Jooles!' as he walked past with Tom Lawson.

'Thanks!' I called after their disappearing backs.

That night—after tea with sponge cake (thanks, Gramma)—I went to Girls Group for the first time. Because she lived near me on Murray Street, Lizzy came to my place so we could walk together. I was glad I didn't have to turn up by myself. We were nearly at the manse when a bunch of boys came toward us and I recognised Rev Friend in front, and Jase and Tom and some older boys from Leaving and Matric, including Michael.

Rev Friend lifted his hand and said, 'Evening, ladies. Enjoy the meeting. She's made chocolate cake for supper so leave some for me!'

Jase smiled at me and said, 'Happy birthday.' Again. The second time that day.

Rev Friend said, 'Well then, no need to save any cake for me! Happy birthday, young lady!'

I smiled my thanks.

They moved on.

Lizzy said, 'Rev Friend takes them down to the Lake to chat. Then we can have the manse to ourselves.'

We sat on the floor around Mrs Friend's coffee table, and she brought out cake with the candles alight and they sang to me. It felt like birthday overload—two cakes *and* two 'happy birthdays' from Jase.

'Now,' said Mrs Friend. 'Because it's Julie's birthday, and her first time along, we'll mix things up a bit. Elizabeth, will you do the honours, please?'

Lizzy passed me a parcel. 'Happy birthday!' everyone said.

I felt hot in the face. This was unexpected. I wasn't used to being the focus of attention. 'Um, thanks.' I picked carefully at the tape.

Mrs Friend said, 'Oh, she's a saver. Me, I'm a ripper—rip, rip, rip the paper!' She laughed.

Was being a saver bad? Mum had a bag of papers she saved to use again. I thought it was what everybody did. Rosie was fidgeting alongside me. Guess she was a ripper, too.

When I got the paper off, there was a Bible, a notebook and a biro. I breathed out, 'Wow!' and sat stunned. No one had ever given me so much for my birthday.

'Look inside, my dear,' said Mrs Friend.

I opened the Bible cover to the first page. She'd written:

To Julie,
    On your birthday 4.9.70
    May you find God in these pages,
    From your Girls Group friends.

And all of them had signed their names. When I looked up it was hard to see them because my eyes were misty. 'Thank you,' was all I could whisper. Definitely birthday overload.

Gracie was right. Mrs Friend sang like an angel. I felt awkward because I didn't know any of the words or what I was supposed to do. It was all new to me; the songs, finding things in the Bible, what Mrs Friend said, what others said. And then the worst—the prayer time. Gracie started and then Rosie, then Suzy, and I realised they were going around the circle, and was I expected to say something? But what could I say? Everyone else had said what I would have. My palms felt sweaty, and my heart was racing. Lizzy was praying and then…

Mrs Friend jumped in and said, 'Thank you, God, that Julie could join us tonight…' and the heat drained out of me. I sucked in breath, blew it out and heard her ask God to be with me on my birthday and always. And then everyone said amen, and it was over.

Chapter Eighteen

Em and I were sitting together at lunch, a rare thing after the rumours started. She was spending more and more of her lunchtimes at the oval—running, hurdling, throwing. I knew she was avoiding me and though I really missed her, I got it. I didn't want to fuel the rumours either.

When I told Em that I was going to church and Girls Group, she said, 'Jesus!'

'Exactly,' I said.

She looked kinda strange at me until she got it.

Then she said, 'Yeah, but really? You? I mean, remember how you said it was in Latin and you couldn't understand it? It's been ages since you went.'

That was true. Old Father O'Day did drone on, and none of the liturgy made sense, even after doing Latin in first and second year. I'd gone because that was what Mum wanted—all her kids lined up along the pew in their Sunday best with shiny, clean faces. No mean feat considering the twins always managed to get themselves filthy just before we walked out the door. Then one day, I'd come into the kitchen still in my pjs and said to Mum that I wasn't going and, somehow, she surprised us both by saying, 'Alright, love.' I'd stayed home every Sunday since, though Mum gave me jobs to do, so it wasn't quite the me-time I'd hoped.

'Not to the RC. I'm going with Liz and Gracie.'

Em looked kinda funny again, like I was someone she didn't know. And I guess that was fair enough—I wasn't sure who I was just then either. But I knew I wanted to find out what it was that Liz and Gracie found so good about their church. Of course, Michael Boston had a lot to do with it. Gracie had adored him since he'd looked out for her in Grade Six. Not that he took advantage at all. He seemed to actually like having her around and treated her as a friend. He was different, was Michael Boston. He was… um… good, somehow. 'Too good to be true,' Gramma used to say, like we should consider anyone guilty until proven innocent.

Em said nothing. She just kept chewing her apple, even though she was down to the core.

I said, 'Yeah, I know, I know… if Justin finds out, it'll be more lies. But I'm bigger than that.'

'Sounds like something your mum'd say.'

That deflated me. I sighed as my shoulders slumped. 'Yeah. It was. Still…' I sat up again and took a deep breath. 'I know who I am.'

Em giggled. 'More Mum-talk?'

Yeah, it was Mum-talk, and it was truth. Mum always spoke truth.

I laughed and punched her arm. Then we noticed Justin

watching us from his group lolling about on the lawn. He made leering eyes and a smushy, kissing face and hugged himself.

Em jumped up. 'I'm gunna practise hurdles. See ya.'

God, when will this ever end?

CANDY BROUGHT her tranny to school. She played it at break times and sang to all the songs. One day, they played *Candy Girl*. She squealed and jumped to her feet. 'This is my song!'

She started singing loudly and badly as she danced around, swivelling her hips, lifting her hair and letting it fall, and making flirty eyes at Justin and his cronies. They smirked and rolled their eyes. For some reason, Justin had never asked her out. I reckon it made her feel second-rate, like being the last one left after sides were picked.

It made me gag to see her act like that. Desperate. Demeaning.

Candy saw me watching and taunted, 'Enjoying the show, girlfriend?'

Lorrie and Skye sniggered.

Justin's friends laughed.

I went inside.

To hide.

THAT NIGHT, I sat on my bed. I opened my Bible to the first page, the one where Mrs Friend had written and the girls had signed their names. I remembered that Mrs Friend had written a verse there. I found Psalm 145:18 and read, *The Lord is near to all who call upon him, to all who call upon him in truth.* Truth.

I read on, *He fulfils the desire of all who fear him, he also hears their cry, and saves them. The Lord preserves all who love him; but all the wicked he will destroy.*

Yeah, bring it on, God! I clenched my teeth and punched the air. Destroy 'em!

Chapter Nineteen

On weekends, Dad and Hans often talked over the back fence. Mostly about gardening, even though Hans said, 'Lil's the gardener really. I just do the hard yakka, like building.' He was building a compost bin in the back corner right over the fence from ours.

'Like me to come round and give you a hand?' asked Dad.

'Know what? That'd be great, actually. I've got a few posts to square up and could do with an extra pair of hands.'

'I'll be there,' said Dad.

'Wouldn't have a long level I could borrow, would you?'

'Sure thing. I'll see you shortly.' Dad turned to me. 'Let Mum know, would ya, Jooles. And then get Patrick to help you clean the chook boxes. Throw it under the lemon tree.'

He disappeared into his shed and emerged moments later with his level and tool bag. 'Back soon.'

Patrick was not thrilled. He whined the whole time. I

was ready to belt him, especially 'cos I didn't like cleaning the chook house either *and* I really wanted to go with Dad. See the Larsen's yard. Maybe see Lily. Maybe.

———

THE NEXT SATURDAY MORNING, Mum was inside baking. The warm, sweet smell drifting out the window made my tummy rumble. Dad's must have, too. He called over the back fence to Hans screwing slats to his compost bin. 'Fiona's baking cake. How about you and Lily come over for a cuppa?'

Hans's head popped up above the fence. He was wearing a dirty toweling hat, and his face was sweaty. He looked at the kids running wild under the sprinkler on the back lawn—it was one of those unseasonably hot October days. He said, 'Thanks anyway. Lil doesn't like to go out much.' He sounded sad.

'How's she getting on?' asked Dad. 'Settling in?'

'Sure is. She loves it here—the peace and quiet after Adelaide.'

'Getting a bit lonely, though?' asked Dad.

Hans looked thoughtful. As if he wasn't sure how much he should say. 'Maybe some.' He stopped there. 'I better get back to it. But thanks for the invite, Barry.' And his head disappeared below the fence.

Chapter Twenty

Dad said I ought to work in the office at Farm Services after I left school. He said they could do with another office girl. I shuddered and screwed up my nose. I reminded him that I was in the A stream and only the Cs, the commercial stream, were the ones who learned typing. Maybe I'd matriculate and go to uni like Em and Jase planned to do, and Rosie McCarthy who wanted to be a lawyer. Mum smiled and nodded at that. She'd always wanted to study more, maybe become a teacher or a doctor, but they'd got married young and had us. I don't think she regretted that but, sometimes, she'd say things like, 'Don't settle down too soon, Julie. Get a good job and enjoy being single for a while. You're a long time married.' And I'd hear a sort of longing in her voice.

'What would you do at uni, Jooles?' Dad asked.

'I dunno. Maybe teaching English or little kids.'

'That'd suit you. You're great with kids.'

We had a Career Day at school where you could find out

what jobs there were and what might suit you. I did a questionnaire and, yeah, teaching was the top of the list. What surprised me was that it said I'd suit architecture and horticulture.

I pondered it all for ages.

Then near the end of Intermediate, I could tell Em was really excited about something but not sure how to tell me. She started sentences three times, sputtering to a stop each time.

'What, Em?' I giggled a bit because she sounded funny and was acting so nervous. 'What is it?'

Finally, she took a deep breath and out it came in a rush like the Crystal Creek in flood, 'I got a sports scholarship at a school in Adelaide, and I go next year, so I won't be here to do leaving or matric, I'm sorry. I'll miss you, Jooles, and…' And there she petered out, I suppose because she saw my mouth was hanging open and I was staring at her, trying to understand what she'd said and what it meant.

We used to talk about what we'd do after school and how we'd go off to uni together. I'd been glad of that because she was always so confident. If I was to go with her, I'd be alright. But by myself? I loved being home and the thought of going away to study in Adelaide made my stomach twist in knots and repel whatever I'd eaten.

I felt betrayed. Abandoned. I blurted, 'You already got it? The sports scholarship. I didn't even know you applied…'

She looked guilty. 'I'm sorry, Jooles, but I didn't want to say in case I didn't get it. It's just that Mr Kipling thought I should apply. He says it'd be a good way to get into sport for a job. That there'd be more opportunities in town than here. And I really want that. You know how much I love track and field.'

I knew, but it didn't make the thought of her leaving any easier. I swallowed. 'So, next year?'

'Yeah. I'll miss you, Jooles.'

She was trying to placate me. Make me see it was for the best. But I was hurt, so the only reply I gave was a nod.

Chapter Twenty-One

One Saturday morning, Dad roped in Patrick and Sean to help him weed the carrots. Said his knees were acting up and he couldn't get down there too well. I wondered. I hoped Dad knew what he was doing—they probably pulled more baby carrots than weeds.

Mum and I were hanging out the washing, and Brigid was sitting in the basket chewing a dolly peg, when Hans and Dad started talking over the fence. Then Dad called us over.

'Hi,' said Hans.

I looked behind him, but Lily wasn't to be seen.

'Hi,' we both said and Mum added, 'Glorious day, isn't it?'

Hans smiled, said, 'Yeah, sure is,' and then, 'I have to go away for a few days this week. Lily'd usually come with me but says she'd rather stay home this time. I don't really like leaving her on her own, but I was wondering if you'd be able to keep an eye out for her? I'd feel happy about her staying then.'

Mum said, 'Is she fine with that? I mean, I don't think we've even met.'

Hans nodded. 'I floated it with her. She seemed to be.'

And so, it was arranged.

A few days later, after Dad got home from work, Mum and I left him with the tribe and went around to the Larsen's. The garden was looking loved, almost as if Em's grandparents still lived there. No roses out yet, but there were bronze-red shoots on the pruned branches, and the lawn was neat and green. Pink geraniums tumbled out of pots on the veranda.

We went to the front door because it was our first time meeting Lily. Our knock sounded hollow, echoing down the passage, as if the house was empty. Maybe Lily had changed her mind and gone with Hans after all. Maybe they didn't have much furniture to absorb the sound. We had to knock twice before the door opened a few inches and Lily's face appeared—her good, left side.

'Hullo,' said Mum. 'I'm Fiona, from over the back fence, and this is my daughter Julie.'

'Oh, yes. Hullo.' Her voice was a bit muffled. She swallowed. 'Sorry, I just sat down to tea.'

'Oh,' said Mum. 'Bad timing, sorry. We just wanted to pop around and see how you're getting on with Hans away.'

'Fine, just fine, thanks.'

While they were talking, I tried to work out how old Lily was. It was a bit hard to see her because, besides her keeping the door half shut, the sun was nearly down, and this side of the house was in shadow. I thought maybe she was twenty, but maybe older like Mrs Newman, our English teacher, who'd had her twenty-fifth birthday that week. The whole time they were talking, Lily never smiled once. And Mum was good at making people smile. I felt sad for her. And for Lily, too.

Mum was saying, 'We'll let you finish your tea, then. I'll pop round in a couple of days, shall I?' Mum wasn't going to give up easily, I could tell.

'Yeah, if you want,' replied Lily in a quiet voice.

I could feel her watching us as we walked down the path.

<hr>

MUM DID GO around a couple of days later. She took scones and actually got to go inside. Lily made them tea that Mum wasn't keen on—dandelion, she thought the jar said—and Lily talked with her about her spinning and weaving and gardening and painting and how she loved the quiet of Yarralinga after the noise of Adelaide.

'Such a lovely, creative girl!' said Mum.

After that, Mum made a habit of visiting Lily at least once a week, even when Hans got back from his trip. She took the little kids, too. She said Lily seemed to like having them there, especially Brigid who was crawling now and pulling herself up on everything.

No, they didn't have kids yet. Maybe soon.

Lily finally opened up to Mum about her face. Mum told Dad and me later. Lily had been in a car accident when she was fourteen. Drunk driver. Her mum and dad were killed. The car caught fire and she didn't get out quick enough. Here she showed Mum down the right side of her face and opened the neck of her shirt to reveal the extent of the scarring.

'Horrible,' Mum told us. 'Poor darling. The accident also made her deaf in her right ear. She doesn't like going out because people stare and think she's stupid because she can't hear very well.'

Dad and I sat and waited while Mum was thinking, staring into her cup of tea. She asked, 'How *do* you forgive someone who's done that to you?' I don't think she expected us to reply. We didn't anyway.

Then she told us that Lily had lived with her grandparents after that, met Hans at art school and they got married. He'd helped her to come to terms with it all, to forgive the driver, and that this was a new start for them.

Yeah, how do *you forgive like that?*

Chapter Twenty-Two

Somehow, Mrs Friend knew the rumours about Em and me. Probably from Mum.

About how kids at school kept on and on with snickering and cruel comments when we went by.

How it made us keep apart when we'd been best friends since forever.

How I missed her.

We never did get to change the name of Girls Group. No one came up with a better alternative and so it stuck. The boys weren't very imaginative either—Boys Group it was.

After we'd sung a bit—I was getting to know some of the songs and didn't feel quite so awkward—we sat around the coffee table for discussion time.

Mrs Friend said, 'Right, I've chosen to call tonight's chat, "Who does God say I am?"' She began talking and reading something from her Bible, but I didn't follow because I was staring at that Bible—it looked so old and well-used with underlinings and notes, some pages loose, dog-eared and a bit grubby on the edges. It was stuffed with so many bits of paper that it must have been twice its original width. I jumped when she said, 'Julie, what do you think?'

I looked blank. I had nothing. 'Sorry?'

'What do you think God thinks about you?'

Me? Why do I have to go first? I was stumped. I mean how would I know? He was God, out there somewhere with more important things to do than think about me, let alone tell me what He thought.

Mrs Friend watched me fumbling for a reply before turning to Gracie. 'How about you, Grace?'

Gracie looked about as understanding of the question as I did.

'Can you tell us about what you used to think of yourself and how you came to change your mind?'

Gracie twigged. 'Oh, yeah, sure.' And she told us about when she hated being a girl and tried to be a boy because her dad said things like 'Stupid girl!' and 'I wish you'd been born a boy' when she did something wrong. And how the boys called her names when she tried to play with them. And even though her Mum had stuck up for her, she still never felt good enough. Until Michael (she giggled and blushed here) had included her and told her she was alright. And how some things had happened that made her dad different and how he now called her his Amazing Grace. She was teary when she reached that bit. Rosie handed her a hanky.

'So,' said Mrs Friend, 'you stopped listening to and believing the hurtful things people said about you.'

'I guess.'

'You stopped telling yourself that you were no good and started loving yourself?'

Gracie nodded. 'Yeah, I did.' She looked a bit embarrassed, as if she shouldn't love herself. As if it wasn't right.

'Right, girls, listen to me. It's really important that you listen to the right voices. To the people who love you and accept you as you are. To love yourself as you are. But you have to choose to do that.' She rested her hand gently on the Bible that was still open on her lap.

'Now, take note of some homework.' She gave us three verses to read and think about that week, verses she said would help us to know what God thought about us. 'And He's the best person to listen to.'

Lizzy asked, 'Do you know, Mrs Friend? Do you know what God says about you?'

Mrs Friend's face went soft. 'Oh, yes, I do. That's why I gave you those particular verses. They've meant a lot to me, you see. One day, I'll tell you my story—how I had to choose to listen to the right voices.'

WHEN I GOT HOME, everyone else was in bed. The kitchen still smelled of Friday fish. It was comforting, so I sat at the kitchen table and opened my Bible's contents page to find the verses that Mrs Friend had given us. John 1:12: *But to all who received him, who believed in his name, he gave power to become children of God.* I copied it into my notebook.

Then I looked for 1 John 3:1. I looked up John 3:1 first and got confused. What did a religious man called

Nicodemus have to do with us? Then I saw the number 1 in front of John and found it was a different part of the Bible.

I copied the first sentence of the verse. *See what love the Father has given us, that we should be called children of God; and so we are.* It was almost the same as the first verse. Maybe that was Mrs Friend's point. To make sure we knew were God's kids.

And then I found the last verse easily, 1 John 4:4 *ff* . What did she mean by *ff*? Fantastic Fridays? Fabulous friends? Forever friends… The smell of fish in my nostrils. Fantastic fish. Forever Friday Fish. Fish on Fridays Forever!

Focus!

I copied verse 4. *Little children, you are of God, and have overcome them; for he who is in you is greater than he who is in the world.*

I thought, *Who are 'them'?* I didn't get it. I read on. *They are of the world, therefore what they say is of the world, and the world listens to them.*

'Oh,' I breathed. *What they say.* People who don't know God. Who aren't God's kids. People who say cruel untruths. Something seemed to flick inside me like a light switch turning on. No, a heater, bright and warm. No, like coming home in winter to find Mum had hot pea-and-ham soup on the table and I was starving. I kept reading as if I was eating that soup, as if I hadn't eaten for a week. I just skipped along the words and phrases I didn't understand, like 'expiation' and 'the day of judgment' until I took a breath at the end of the chapter. Then, I went back to read something that had tugged my heart to stop reading, but I'd ignored. *Whoever confesses that Jesus is the Son of God, God abides in him, and he in God.*

And I knew that I wanted more than anything to be one of God's kids and overcome the lies and people who said them.

Chapter Twenty-Three

I took ages to get to sleep. I couldn't stop giggling and hugging myself and crying. And whispering, 'Thank you, thank you, God,' over and over. I wanted to shout and sing, but that would've woken Maria and Kathleen and probably Mum, too. She was a light sleeper, always attuned to any kid waking up.

Then, suddenly, it was Saturday morning, and I could hear everyone already at the breakfast table. I'd slept in.

'Morning,' sang Mum as I went into the kitchen. 'Did you have nice time at Girls Group?'

'It was great!' How could I say what had happened? Did it really happen? I felt different. Did I look different?

But Mum didn't expect any more. She went on buttering toast for Aiden and James. She handed me a bib to tie around Brigid's neck. 'Here, love,' she said to me, 'Take over, would you?'

I sat down next to my littlest sister and picked up her spoon. Usually, Miss Independence fought me for it because she wanted to feed herself, and she could. Kind of. It's just that Mum didn't want the extra job of cleaning porridge off the floor. But this morning, Brigid sat still and stared at me for so long as if she could see right inside me. Then she smiled like the sun and reached out her arms to hug around my neck.

I hugged her back. 'I love you, too, baby.' When she let go, she sat back calmly and waited for me to feed her. Wonder of wonders!

Dad was waiting on the back veranda when I went outside. He said, 'We'll set the tomatoes out this morning, Jooles.' His seedling pots were lined up, ready.

'Is it alright if I go round to see Mrs Friend first?'

Dad was a bit taken aback. Saturdays were our days together in the garden. This particular Saturday was perfect spring weather.

'Well, I s'pose, girlie. You were there last night, though.' I could see he was disappointed.

'Yeah, but I want to tell her something important. I won't be long.' I kissed his cheek and left before he could make a reply, got on my bike and rode fast down Wattle Street to the manse on the corner.

When Mrs Friend opened the door, I rushed to her and buried myself against her. I nearly knocked her flying, but she steadied and wrapped her arms around me tightly.

'Julie! Whatever's the matter? Is it your mum? One of the children.'

My voice was muffled because my face was buried in her cardi. It smelled like eucalyptus. Clean and fresh. 'Thank you. Just thank you.'

She clasped my shoulders then and pulled me out of the

hug. She looked at me and smiled. 'Oh,' she breathed. 'Oh. You believe, don't you?'

Her face misted over, and I realised there were tears in my eyes. Maybe in hers, too. I nodded.

'Come in. Come in. I want to hear all about it. This is truly wonderful.'

NEXT DAY, as we sat at the breakfast table—boiled eggs and toast fingers for Sundays—Mum said, 'You seem very happy, Julie. Good to see.'

'Must be in love, eh, Fiona?' said Dad. He thought he was making a joke.

'Maybe she is,' said Mum.

'Who's the lucky boy?' He winked at me.

Patrick wolf whistled. He'd just learned how.

I grinned and said nothing.

I looked at the clock.

Dad released me. 'Off you go then. Enjoy church.'

WHEN I PLUCKED up courage to tell Em that I was a Christian now, she just nodded and said, 'Mmm. Guess you'll be going to church all the time now.' I wanted to say, 'Come with me,' but the words got caught in my throat.

It was easier to tell Jase. I guess because he went to the Rev's Boys Group, he understood more than Em.

'That's great, Jooles,' he simply said and gave me a smile that warmed me to my toes. He added, 'So, we might see you at combined group nights a bit more, yeah? And at church?' My toes melted in my shoes.

Yeah, he wasn't all gushy about it like Gracie, Liz and Rosie were. They jumped up and down and hugged me, laughing and squealing like they'd won the grand finals. I was glad Justin and Co were nowhere in sight.

I thought it would be easy at school after that, that God would stop the jibes and gossip and taunts. I asked Mrs Friend, 'Isn't being a Christian s'posed to make it easier? But they're still at it. Why do the lies keep going?'

'Sometimes, Julie,' she replied, 'God isn't interested in us having an easy life. Sometimes, he has bigger plans for us, and we have to go through the tough situations to learn those plans.'

I wasn't comforted by that. I just wanted God to do a number on all the liars because now it felt as if the rumours were accepted as truth. How could we change that? When would it end? Was it slander or libel? I could never remember which was written and which was spoken.

Whatever, it went on and on through the rest of the year, whispering behind hands and bare-faced taunts when Em and I went by. I was glad when we were let out for Christmas holidays.

Just before Christmas, I was coming out of the butcher's. Lily was sitting in their car waiting for Hans who was in Crisp's Hardware. Mrs Hawkins and Mrs Vincent were standing outside gossiping away. They didn't see me. They were pretending not to look at Lily. I think she saw them because she ducked her head so that her hair fell across her face.

Mrs Hawkins said, 'Strange one, that girl.' Then, in a condescending tone, 'I guess she must feel bad about her kids getting burned. Guilt does that, you know.'

I lost it then. The untruths. The meanness. The injustice. I strode up to them and looked straight at Mrs Hawkins. My anger spewed out. 'Stop it! You wicked old witch!' (Yeah, well maybe it was the 'b' word.) 'Why don't you ask them what happened instead of making up lies?'

Mrs Hawkins eyes flew open wide. 'Well, I never!' she exclaimed and sucked in her cheeks.

I didn't wait for more. I plonked the meat parcel in my carry basket and pedalled away fast.

MUM WASN'T VERY happy about my outburst when she heard that I had been 'extremely rude' to Mrs Hawkins.

I wasn't sure about Gramma Kent. She had her back to us, hovering over the apricot jam on the stove, pretending not to be involved.

Mum had her arms folded tight. 'I'm not going to make you go and apologise, Julie, but it was wrong.'

'But, Mum, she's always saying mean things, making up lies about people. Gossiping. You should hear her!'

Gramma made an agreeing noise into the jam.

Mum said, 'Oh, I have, my dear. But perhaps you went about it the wrong way.'

'Why? Someone's got to stop her! Nasty, old biddy!'

Gramma snorted and turned slightly. 'Don't you worry,

Julie girl, Mrs Hawkins'll get her comeuppance.' She stirred the jam so vigorously that some of it spattered onto her arm. She gasped and ran for the cold butter.

What did Gramma know that I didn't? I did remember that she'd gone to school with Mrs Hawkins forever ago. What happened then, I wondered?

Mum wouldn't back down. I stomped to my room and fell on the bed, hitting my head on my Bible and jabbing myself with the pen. That made me even more cranky. Bible bashing! Huh!

I laid there for a bit and then pulled the notebook from where I'd closed it in the Bible. It fell open where I'd written out Psalm 145. I read it again. *The Lord is near to all who call on him, to all who call on him in truth.* Truth. Not lies. Truth.

He fulfils the desire of all who fear him, he also hears their cry, and saves them. The Lord preserves all who love him; but all the wicked he will destroy.

I thought about what Mum'd said. Was it the wrong way? Did I change anything? Well, perhaps. Maybe Mrs Hawkins knew now that she was wrong. Maybe? Maybe not. I didn't know. Was it my job to shut the lies up? King David didn't think so. He said God would do that.

I sighed. *God, I'm calling on you to preserve our lives, Lily's and Em's and mine, when people speak mean lies about us.*

Later, I asked Mrs Friend about 'calling on God in truth', what it meant. She gave me another verse to look up—John 14:6. I wrote in my notebook. *Jesus said to him, 'I am the way, and the truth, and the life; no one comes to the Father, but by me.'* I tried to puzzle that one through, starting at Jesus being truth.

Chapter Twenty-Four

It was Christmas Eve. Mum and I, Maria, Kathleen and Brigid were over at the Price's making Christmas lebkuchen with Mrs Price and Em. It was crowded in their kitchen and a bit of an obstacle course because Brigid, now one and walking, kept popping up next to us and tripping us over.

Finally, Mum sat next to Oma with Brigid on her lap and watched us roll and cut and cook. Maria and Kathleen seemed to be eating more dough than they were rolling and cutting for cooking. Oma kept giving directions in German. Mrs Price was trying to be patient, but she was getting hot in the face—more than putting trays in and out of the oven should have caused.

Brigid offered her lebkuchen to Oma.

Oma smiled at Brigid. 'Danke.'

Brigid said, 'Da-da.'

'Did you hear that? Her first German word!' exclaimed Mrs Price.

Jase and Tom came in, swiped some hot biscuits and headed out the back screen door with a 'Thanks, Mrs Price' from Tom. Maria and Kathleen followed after Jase like puppies. I would've liked to follow, too. I watched him turn and say 'Boo!' to them. They squealed, and he chased them around the geraniums until Maria turned and said 'Boo!' to him. He laughed loudly, and the girls giggled. I giggled, too.

Mum looked up at me from the dough she was rolling. She had that dead-pan face that Em and Jase did some-times. The one I called The Look. She dropped her head, but I saw crinkles at the corners of her eyes, and her lips twitched. I felt my face go hot. *What? What's so funny? I'm only laughing at the girls.*

Mum picked up a star cutter and asked, 'So, Emily, how are you feeling about next year?'

Em beamed. 'Can't wait!' Then she tried to tone it down a bit. 'I'll be able to train lots more and go to carnival days...' She glanced at me and trailed off, obviously not wanting to sound too excited.

But it was alright. I was alright. I mean, I'd miss her, but it was going to be good for her dreams.

Mum, Dad and I were invited for Jase and Em's sixteenth birthday tea on January sixth. Mrs Price served Sweet and Sour Chicken Casserole and rice. Em's oma was poking the pineapple to the side of her plate with a look of distaste.

I heard Dad mutter to Mum, 'Pineapple is for dessert!'

Mum elbowed him and her face tinged with pink. She

said loudly, 'This is lovely, Ruth. Where did you find the recipe?'

'Thank you, Fiona. It's from last week's *Women's Weekly* lift-out. Good to try something new, don't you think?'

'Yes, it is,' said Mum with emphasis. She turned slightly to Dad. 'I'm going to give it a go next week.'

Dad groaned quietly, but then turned the groan into a sort of burp. 'Excuse me! Er… yes, very nice, Ruth. Very nice.'

I looked at Em and Jase. They were trying to hold it together, too. Em was squinting at her plate and Jase's lips were sealed tight. He managed to say, 'Nice, Mum. Thanks,' before he had to clamp his lips together again.

Awkward silence.

Mum said, 'So, Brian, how's the shop going?'

Dad latched on like a drowning man. 'Yeah, mate, I hear you're doing some upgrading.'

'Too right,' said Mr Price. 'Time we got a bit more modern…'

And everyone breathed again as the conversation steered into safe waters.

When we were enjoying the birthday cake (Apricot Nectar Cheesecake—Dad asked for seconds) Dad said to Jase and Em, 'So, guess you'll be going for your L's then?'

Jase nodded. 'Yep, I will be, next week.'

Even though Em was off to Adelaide and had decided not to get her licence yet, they'd been studying the road rules together and, sometimes, I quizzed them. Jase would pass fine and then be learning to drive. Already, their dad had taken him out on the back roads to practise.

We went out for a walk after tea, leaving the adults

talking—dads about sport, mums about recipes. When we were heading out the door, I heard Mum say to Mrs Price, 'I don't try much different. Hard enough just doing the usuals for my tribe, though Jooles is a great help. She does a lot of cooking now.'

I felt a warm glow. *Thanks, Mum.* I looked at Jase to see if he'd heard. He was busy pulling three-corner jacks out of his thongs… so maybe not.

The sun was sinking toward the hills. We headed west on Sturt Street, over Redbank Road and then to Crystal Lake. The gums that lined the lake cut long shadows across the paddock. In between, the sun shone through the spent seed-heads of wild oats, making them glow like a myriad of dancing lanterns. It was my favourite time of a summer's day.

There was the sound of a bike bell behind us. 'Yar, me hearties!' Larry rode up and skidded next to us, sending dirt over Em's feet. She scowled at him. He took no notice. 'So, I hear you're coming to live with me, Em, my girl. Pretty cool!'

She scowled again. 'First, I'm not your girl and second, it's not your place. It's Aunty Sue's even if you do live with them.'

He grinned. 'Yeah, yeah, yeah. Anyways, can't wait to show you round, introduce you to my boys.'

Jase spoke up then, 'If you do anything to hurt my sister, I'll…'

'You'll what, boy? You and your girlfriend, eh? What'll you do?' Larry snorted. 'I just wanna show her a good time, is all.'

'Just rack off, Larry.'

And he did—turned his bike toward the dam wall and peddled away. Laughing.

'You gotta watch out for him, Em,' said Jase. He's bad. I wish you didn't have to stay at Aunty Sue's with him there.'

'I know. But I'll keep out of his way. Plenty to do with school and training.'

We walked on. Neither of them mentioned whether they'd noticed Larry's 'you and your girlfriend'. But I had. I held it like a prize.

Chapter Twenty-Five

Term 1, Leaving

It was like I could breathe again when school went back and I found out that Justin Waters had left to work on the farm. Lots of his friends had, too, because they didn't want to go to uni.

The rumours gradually faded, and Candy and Co almost ignored me. They had something else to focus on—a new guy from Maud Springs whose parents decided he needed a new start away from his old school but didn't want to send him to Adelaide. They drove him across every day, so he didn't have to go on the bus. He was different. Candy and Co picked on him mercilessly when the teachers were out of hearing. Even though I was glad not to bear the brunt of their whip-sharp tongues, I felt sorry for him. Jase, Tom and Pete May tried to befriend him, but he seemed so beaten about that he clammed up and didn't look at or talk to anyone. Even the teachers gave up trying to get him to answer.

They weren't the only changes though. Gracie wandered around in a daze half the time because Michael Boston had gone off to Adelaide Uni. She said he was just a friend but, yeah, you know.

And then there was Em, or rather there wasn't. I'd gone with her family to wave her off on the Adelaide train a week before school went back. I'd promised to write (care of Mrs S. Price) and she said she'd be home to visit in a few weeks. She was excited, but nervous too, I could tell. When the train was out of sight, I kissed the silver half-heart on its chain around my neck, our present to each other at Christmas, and swiped at my eyes. There was a hollow feeling in and around me.

No one said anything. Mrs Price put her arm around my shoulders as we all just sort of drifted away from the station. I could hear her sniffling. Jase got on his bike and rode off fast. Guess he didn't want to be around our sad faces or, just maybe, he would have cried too. Em always said that being a twin was a special bond, and so I guessed he'd miss her even more than I would.

———

'HERE, Jooles, can you take these over to the Price's?' Dad handed me a basket of late tomatoes, beans and peaches. He stooped down and picked a cucumber to add to the pile.

'Thanks Dad,' I said. I knew he was giving me a reason to go visit the Price's and ask about Em.

I said 'Tag' to Em's Oma on the veranda and then called,

'Hullo,' as I went down the hallway into the kitchen. Mrs Price was sitting at the table holding a letter.

'Hullo, Julie. Here, have a seat.' She pulled the table-cloth across to the end of the table. The sauce and Vegemite, sugar bowl and bread box slid with it.

I put my basket on the table and sat next to her.

'Thanks for those. My beans are all finished now.' She held up the letter. 'It's from Emily.'

'Is she alright?' I asked. 'I haven't had a letter for ages.'

'We don't get many either, I'm afraid. Here, you can read it.' She passed it over and got up to stir something sweet smelling that was bubbling on the stove. Fig jam, I think.

For a letter from Em, it was sparse, considering how good she was with words. Only one side of a page, the words large and spread out with wide gaps between the lines. When I got to the *Love from Emily* at the bottom, I thought, what did she say, really? Nothing much at all. She practised track and field before classes, then out at the oval at lunch, more training after school, then home to her Aunty Sue's for tea and homework. But there was nothing about fun stuff at weekends, or friends, or how she felt about it all, or even about missing home.

'Thanks,' I said to Mrs Price as I slid the letter back into the envelope and stood.

Em's mum turned from the stove. 'Has she said any more to you, Julie?' She sounded hopeful.

'No, not really. I mean I've only got a couple of letters and it's been a month since the last one. She just says she's missing everyone but training hard. I hope she's alright.'

Em's mum nodded once. Her shoulders dropped. 'I miss her so much. I hope she knows that.'

I was surprised at that. Em'd told me that she didn't think her mum even knew she was there half the time. But I said, 'I'm sure she does, Mrs Price.' I went to her and gave her a quick hug, not like Mum would have given, but a hug all the same.

'Oh, thank you, my dear! I guess you miss her, too, huh?'

I could feel the tears stinging behind my eyes, so I said, 'Better go. I'll get the basket later,' and fled down the hallway. I pulled up short as Jase came out of the front room and nearly collided with me. 'Sorry!'

'No, sorry!' he said. 'My fault.' He saw my eyes then. 'You alright?'

I cleared my throat and mumbled a bit about just talking to his mum and reading Em's letter and missing her and then the tears really came. And I let them because it was Jase standing there and he was Em's twin and he would understand.

He swayed from foot to foot. He ran a hand through his hair, reached toward me, but then slid both of his hands into his pockets. 'Yeah,' he said. 'Me, too.' He blew out a breath.

My nose was running, but I didn't have a hanky. I sniffed.

He noticed and said, 'I'll grab you one of Em's.' He moved toward her door. He wasn't blocking my exit anymore.

'Don't worry. I'll get one at home,' I called as I raced out the front door and down the steps.

'Tschüss,' Oma called after me.

PART VI
EMILY

Chapter Twenty-Six

Term 2, ADELAIDE

Saturday night. I sat on my bed. Streetlight leaked in around the drawn blind. I didn't want to stay up with Aunty Sue anymore doing her 5,000-piece jigsaw of a Cotswold's cottage garden, and I didn't want her horrid, yappy terrier trying to mount my foot again. Once, Aunty Sue saw me uncross my legs to get away from him and thought I was kicking her precious dog. She was grumpy-angry at me for days after. Huh! I wished I had!

Larry was out with his friends. He'd asked me again to go, but I didn't know if I wanted to hang out with them and do the dumb stuff they did.

I missed home so much. Hollow inside. Empty. It was so grey and cold. I was so grey and cold. It was worse that it was winter, dripping and wet and grey and cold. Always cold. I saw little spoggies on the bare peach-tree branch, so cold they were huddling into each other and sort of chirpy-crying. I wanted to cuddle them. I was so lonely for Mum and Dad and Jase. And most of all for Jooles. If she was here feeling like this, she'd write a poem about it, about how it felt.

I opened the desk drawer and took out the compendium that Mum gave me last Christmas before I left. I unzipped it right around three sides and laid it flat. The smell from the paper, like Grandma's roses, hit my nostrils and straight away it was summer when I was little, back in her garden playing under the sprinkler on the front lawn with Jase and Jooles and roses all around. I cried like the sprinkler then.

When I got myself together again and cleared my nose, I wrote *Dear Jooles*. But instead of words to her, I started writing about the little spoggies chirping sadly. I couldn't make it rhyme like a poem was supposed to. I signed it, *Missing you, Em xxx*, folded it and put it in an envelope addressed to Jooles. She would understand.

> Homesick
> It is growing very cold outside.
> The chubby sparrows huddle close to one
>   another
> and chirrup dejectedly.
> The rain begins to drift
> in a damp, non-ceasing cloud.
> The grey is permanent
> and very dull.
> The time of day means little
> for the night will be the same.
> The rain goes on, and on, and on
> Like my tears.

JOOLES WROTE BACK STRAIGHT AWAY. She's a good friend. My best friend.

Dear Em,

I miss you so much. There's been a lot of rain here, too. And the spoggies here are shivering. They sound like they have colds, the way they sort of cough-cheep. I really like your poem—I can hear how you feel when I read it. I'm sorry you're so homesick and I wish you were here. I'm glad you didn't try to make it rhyme because I think free verse is so much better!

I hope you don't mind, but I added some more. What do you think?

> But wait.
> For God,
> knowing how heavy the cold oppresses,
> opens up the cloud and sends
> a warmer messenger,
> so we may dream of times to come.
> And in that brief moment
> the crystal drips from the blade of grass.

I wanted to add that bit about God, Em. I pray for you to find Him and be happy. Can't wait till you come home.

Missing you so much,

Jooles xxx

'Huh!' I breathed. I was a bit put out first to see she'd

added to it. But it showed she really understood. I could tell she was still going to Mrs Friend's group, talking about God like that. I read it again and again with my first verse. Maybe she *had* made it better.

I thought about what she said. How she prayed for me to find God and be happy. What did that mean anyway? I had no idea where you even look for something that you can't see. And how do you know that you've found Him? And why would that make me happy? I needed to get out of this prison of a house and have some fun. Find some friends.

LAST AGAIN. Always last. Even in my best event, 800 m, I couldn't get past fourth. And they never used my name or included me in anything. 'Hey, country kid. Go home. We got this.' I know they purposely made me fumble the baton, so I dropped it. Then they dropped me from the team. And the names kept coming. 'Skinny Emmy' and 'Baby face'. Not very imaginative but cruelly spoken. I felt ripped to shreds.

I decided not to spend another cold, lonely night at Aunty Sue's. I told Larry I'd go out with him and his friends.

'HI,' said the boy leaning in close. Beer breath. 'Who's this?'

'No one,' said Larry. 'Cousin. She's into girls.'

'What? Am not! Who told you that?'

'Dunno. Just heard.'

'And you believe everything you 'just heard'?' *I'll show you!*

I turned and stepped close to the boy, so close that my boob brushed his arm.

'Hi,' I said. 'Don't listen to my loser cousin. I'm Em and I'm into boys.'

———

JIMMY INVITED me to the drive-in.

'Only if it's *Love Story*,' I said.

'I was thinking *Airport*. But yeah, right, if you want.'

We went in his dad's Monaro.

Jimmy ran his hand up my thigh.

'Let's get in the back,' he said.

I really want to see the film, I thought. 'Alright,' I said.

He pulled the seat forward for us to climb over.

———

AT INTERMISSION, I didn't want to get out and see people, pretend that nothing had happened. Jimmy went off to get some drinks, and I could see him laughing with some of his mates. They were slapping him on the back. Larry, too—he looked back at the car.

I hunkered down below the front seat, feeling burning heat rise up my throat and cheeks.

PART VII
JOOLES

Chapter Twenty-Seven

Term 2, YARRALINGA

Rev and Mrs Friend arranged for the boys' and girls' groups to meet together—about fourteen of us. It was a frosty Friday night. They'd got a few dads to build a bonfire down by Crystal Lake and sent us off to find ourselves a long, smooth gumtree stick. We made damper dough that we rolled around the stick and held over the hot coals. Our faces glowed and burned with the heat. Our backs chilled and shivered with the cold.

'Bugger!' said Pete as his damper slid off into the fire. We laughed, then didn't. 'Oh, sorry! Pardon my French,' he mumbled to Mrs Friend.

She said nothing. Her eyes twinkled. She handed him her own stick and turned to roll dough on another for herself. The Rev raked Pete's damper to the side. The burning smell had us constantly checking to see if ours were still secure. We filled them with butter and honey and hungrily ate them, slurping the deliciousness that dripped from the ends, and drinking hot Milo from Mrs Friend's thermos flasks.

After we'd cleaned up, Mrs Friend brought out her guitar. I was surprised when Jase picked up a guitar, too. I had no idea he was learning to play. They fiddled around a bit making sure their guitars were in tune together, and then Mrs Friend led us in singing. Jase didn't sing—he was concentrating on his fingers making chords. I felt proud of him.

I knew most of the words now. The Rev's voice was deep and warm and strong. I reckon Mum and Dad could have heard him from home.

Mrs Friend's strumming faded. Jase's followed. The Rev said, 'Let's just sit quietly for a while. No speaking. Just close your eyes and listen.'

I closed my eyes. I remembered doing this game in Grade 1. 'How many different sounds can you hear?' the teacher had said. I checked off sounds on my fingers: the bob-bob of frogs, a bird disturbed in sleep, a plover's shrill call, a lamb bleating in the distance and its mother's answer, a car driving out of town toward Redbank, sparks from the fire. That last sound was so sudden and sharp that I opened my eyes in time to see the red shower falling. Then I saw Jase across the fire. His eyes were open, shining with firelight, and he was looking at me. Maybe the damper and honey reached my stomach just then because I suddenly felt warm inside. I held his gaze.

The Rev began to pray. 'Our Father, who art in heaven…'

Caught out, I quickly shut my eyes, ducked my head and joined in.

Chapter Twenty-Eight

At the beginning of Term 3, I came into the kitchen to find Mum on her knees drawing around Sean's foot as he stood on a piece of cardboard.

'Ah, Julie,' she said. 'I have to go to town for an appointment on Friday. Would you like to come? It'd be alright to miss school for a day.'

I jumped at that. Would I ever!

'I've already asked Mrs Price's permission for Emily to meet us in Rundle Street and spend the day with us. Emily's said she would.'

We caught the train down early Friday morning and watched the sun rise above the hills as we rattled along. I was really excited—both for a day in Adelaide with Mum, and to hang out with Em. It seemed ages since she'd come home to visit.

We walked out of the station and up to Beehive Corner. Em was already there staring in Darrell Lea's window at the mountains of every kind of chocolate imaginable, and peanut brittle and coconut ice stacked in pyramids, and boiled sweets in their shiny jars. The smell of licorice and chocolate wafted out the open door. My mouth began to water.

I snuck up behind Em and put my hands over her eyes. She jumped and laughed, turned and hugged me.

Mum laughed, too. 'Hi, Emily. I'm so glad you could meet us.' She gave Em one of her mother-hugs. Then another, saying, 'This one's from your mum.'

'Thanks, Mrs Kent,' said Em and grinned from ear to ear.

Mum breathed in deeply. 'Mmmm, I love that smell. Do you want something? How about some licorice allsorts? Or one of those marshmallows?' She pointed to the hill of them piled high, coconut bristling in the chocolate coating.

She started for the entry, but Em said, 'No thanks, Mrs Price. I just had breakfast.'

Mum stopped. 'Oh, alright then. Julie?'

What could I say? I would love one, but wouldn't it look a bit wrong to eat it in front of Em? 'No, I'm good thanks, Mum.'

Mum looked disappointed. 'Oh, well, I'll get some things on the way to the train later. You know how Dad loves those licorice bullets.' And so did she.

Mum excused herself then and went off to her appointment on North Terrace, telling us to meet her right back there at twelve sharp so we could get some lunch together. We headed off down Rundle Street, ambling along, window shopping and chatting about everything and anything that was happening in Yarralinga. Em was like a sponge soaking it all in.

We slid our plastic trays along the shelf in Coles Cafeteria and chose our lunch. Pasties for me and Mum. Em's hand hovered before she chose a plain cheese sandwich.

'It's fine, Em,' said Mum. 'Have what you want. I'm paying today.'

'Thanks, Mrs Kent, but I'm not very hungry. This looks good.'

We chose our drinks, and Mum paid while we collected our cutlery, sauce and serviettes, and then slid into a booth.

'Yum!' I said as I squirted sauce on my pasty. I took a big mouthful and right away knew I'd made the best choice.

Em was quiet beside me. She fiddled with her sandwich, picked a tiny bit off and put it in her mouth.

Mum said, 'Are you alright, Emily?'

'Yeah, fine. Bit of a tummy bug, that's all.' She sipped her lemonade.

Mum frowned but didn't say anything. We ate in silence for a bit and then Mum asked, 'So, how's school, Emily? Made some friends?'

Em sighed at that. 'No. It's hard being new when there's all these groups and they've known each other from the start. There's one girl from up the River somewhere who's nice. But she's on a different scholarship—Arts, I think— and so we don't have many classes together.'

I watched her nudge the sandwich around the plate. Her fingernails were bitten down—something she'd never done before. She sounded so sad, and I felt so helpless.

'I'm sorry that's the case,' said Mum. 'I hope it changes for you soon.'

Em nodded and took another sip of her lemonade.

When we finished, Mum suggested that we spend more time together while she did some shopping. 'I need to get the boys' shoes.' She pulled the cardboard outlines of Sean's and Conal's feet from her bag. 'I'll meet you at four-thirty at Beehive Corner. Alright, girls?'

Only when we were walking down North Terrace did Em tell me about how hard it was living with her aunt and uncle. When I asked about Larry being there too, she went red and said that her aunt and uncle had kicked him out because he kept coming home drunk, late at night. Then she started talking about school, how she was bullied by the other girls. The names and snide comments were almost as bad as Justin's lies and Candy's cruel sarcasm.

'Please, don't tell Mum and Dad, and especially not Jase. Please Jooles. I couldn't bear them to know. Mum and Dad'd make me go home to Yarralinga and I need to keep doing sport here. To get better at it.'

'Even if it's so horrible?'

'Mmm,' she said. 'I can do this.'

'Sounds like mum-talk to me,' I threw back at her.

She got it, and actually smiled. 'Yeah, I know. I know.' She was quiet for a bit. 'Sometimes, though, I don't know if I'll ever be good enough. You know, back home, Mr Kipling said I had what it takes. But here it's like there's so many others who are really good and I feel like the bottom of the pile half the time. Not fast enough. Not fit enough. Not strong enough.'

I didn't know what to say that would make it alright for her. Mrs Friend would've known. But she wasn't there to tell me. All I could say was, 'Well, I think you're great at sport, Em, and one day, I'll see you on the telly winning gold!'

Even though we were out on North Terrace with people strolling around us, she put her arm around me and pulled me to her side. 'You're the *best* friend, Jooles! My *best* friend!' She pulled the silver half-heart from under her shirt and held it up. I pulled out mine.

'Snap!' we said together and laughed. We linked pinkies like we used to as kids and made a wish. Then we turned toward the Art Gallery.

Chapter Twenty-Nine

We spent the rest of the afternoon in the Gallery with its high-ceilinged halls and old paintings in their fancy frames. We gazed at landscapes and giggled over nudes until we came through an archway into another room where a huge sculpture stood in the middle. It was so beautiful that I stopped. Em ran into me, and then, coming around me, stopped, too. We stood gaping.

It was carved from stone—marble, I think—of a young girl dancing. The sculptor had caught her spinning motion perfectly in her hair and the long, fluid skirt. Her smooth, bare arms reached skyward. Her face was upturned and full of joy and adoration. And it was then that I remembered the look I'd seen on Lily Larsen's face, upturned to Hans's kiss, full of adoration. Gratitude.

Finally, I let go my breath. 'Wow!'

'Yeah, wow! So beautiful!' whispered Em.

We moved around the girl, looking from every angle. I

felt she could dance off the plinth and pirouette out the door. Laughing as she went. Or singing.

I went to the plinth to read the plaque and gaped again.

'Em! Look!'

There was written: Hans LARSEN born Glenelg 1945, GRATITUDE 1968, Marble, Gift of the sculptor.

'That's *our* Hans Larsen! Oh, wow!'

'Wait till I tell everyone back home!'

We must have been getting a bit loud because the Gallery guard who was sitting in the corner cleared his throat and frowned. Then he got up and came toward us.

'Voices down, please, ladies. You like that one?'

We nodded.

'Me, too,' he said. 'This is the best part of my job, sitting in this room where I can see it and the reactions of people when they come through that arch.' He looked up at the dancer and scratched his bristly, grey beard. 'She makes this old guy's heart happy.'

'We know him,' I blurted.

'Who?'

'Hans. The sculptor. He lives over my back fence.'

'They bought my Grandad's house,' added Em.

'Well, how about that! Small world, eh? He's quite famous you know. Got work in all the major galleries and some hotel foyers, too. But I think this is his best.'

WE TOLD MUM ABOUT IT. 'Oh, my goodness! Fancy that!' she said. 'Well, that'll stop a few gossips back home.'

'Yeah,' said Em, 'including my dad.'

Em's bus came along before I'd said goodbye properly. She looked out the window, a sad, pale face and a faint wave. If she smiled, I missed it. Mum put her arm around my shoulders, and we went into Darrell Lea and bought up big on licorice and Rocklea Road. Then we went to catch the train.

We talked about our day and mostly about Em. Mum was concerned and said things like, 'She didn't eat much. Looking a bit thin, too. Maybe the sport is too much for her. Mmm, she didn't look at all well.'

When we got home, she said to Dad, 'Looks a bit peaky. Homesick, I think. I'll have a word with Ruth.'

'Right-e-o, love,' Dad said absently. He looked frazzled after his evening feeding the kids and getting them to bed.

***

I DECIDED to write to Em every week, to tell her she was still my best friend, even if I did have other friends and went to Girls Group. I'd write about all that was happening in Yarralinga, at school, and maybe about Girls Group, too. And about the basketball (oh, yeah, called *netball*, now) and how the team really missed her and hadn't made the finals this year. Anything and everything, I'd tell her.

And I did. Not one letter, but four long letters. One every week.

But I didn't get a reply. Not one.

One afternoon, Jase and I were unlocking our bikes at the same time, so I wheeled alongside him. 'Hi, Jase.'

He grinned. 'Hi, Jooles. How's it going?'

I couldn't help but smile back. 'Yeah, good thanks. Ummm, can I ask you something?'

'Sure,' he said.

'What's with Em? I've written all these letters since I saw her in Adelaide, and she hasn't written back. Is she still at your aunty's?'

Jase turned to look straight ahead, but I could see his face had changed—sort of frozen and pale. *Is he sick, too?* And his eyes were wider than usual. Such nice brown eyes. He had the same thick, dark lashes as Em.

He swallowed. 'Umm, yeah. Still at Aunty Sue's.'

'Oh.' *So why hasn't she written back?* I had thought about asking for their Aunty Sue's phone number but canned that idea. I mean, I didn't want to ask Mum and Dad to pay for the STD call, and even if I did ring, what if I got her aunty or uncle? Then I'd have to wait for her to get to the phone. That'd really be wasting money.

'Is she alright, Jase? I mean, I know she's missing home and all, but do you know if she's alright? Is she sick or something?'

'Yeah, I think she's not feeling too good. Guess she's just busy with school and training and stuff. Well, gotta go. Need to help Uncle Ken at the shop. Be seein' you.'

He pushed off and rode away before I could reply.

Suddenly, I had a memory of Candy and Co snickering about a girl in the B class who'd left school in the middle of first term. They'd used a phrase I'd not heard before: up the duff. I swatted the memory away, but not before a feeling of dread settled in my stomach.

I GOT HOME from school to find Mrs Price sitting at the table with Mum. She was hunched over a mug of cold tea. The milk was congealing on the top. She didn't look up but I could see she'd been crying, and she was clutching a soggy hanky in her hand.

'Hi, Julie, give us some time, will you?' said Mum. 'Can you get the kids outside for a bit? They're all in the sitting room.'

Unnecessary—I could hear them galumphing around like elephants. I herded them outside.

That night, when the others were in bed, Mum took me into the sitting room and sat next to me on the lounge. She ummed and cleared her throat a couple of times and sighed and ummed again.

Finally, she said, 'Julie, you won't be able write to Emily for a while, dear. Or hear from her either.'

'Why?'

'You mustn't breathe a word of this to anyone. Yes?'

'Al-right?'

'Mrs Price had a call from Emily's Aunt Susan, where she's boarding. Do you remember how she didn't look well when we saw her in town?'

'Yes,' I whispered, dreading what Mum would say next. Hoping she wouldn't.

But she did. 'Emily is pregnant.'

A sick feeling rushed into my stomach. My face went cold. The sick feeling climbed to my throat. I clutched my arms across my belly and hugged tight, willing it away, breathing it away with big, gulping breaths. With every exhale came, 'Oh, Em!'

Mum's arm went around my shoulders. 'I'm sorry, dear. I'm so sorry.'

When my breaths slowed again, I whispered, 'What'll happen to her? Will she come home?' But I knew that wouldn't happen. I could imagine the horrible gossip and what it would do to her, and her mum and dad. And Jase.

'No. I'm going to go down to town in a few days with Mrs Price to organise for Emily to go into Kate Cocks Memorial Babies' Home.'

I'd never heard of it.

'It's a place for single girls to live until they have their babies.'

'And then…?'

'I don't know.'

'The baby…?'

Mum had tears in her eyes now. She brushed at her cheeks and sniffed. 'She can't keep it, Julie.'

I turned into Mum's embrace and sobbed. I thought of all Em's dreams lying broken and trampled at her feet. *What have you done, Em? What have you done?*

I DIDN'T KNOW how to talk to Jase after I heard. I mean, he must've known. But how do you let someone know that you know something like that. Even though I'd promised Mum that I wouldn't say anything, it was Jase. Surely it'd be alright to talk to him. But what would we say anyway? Nothing that'd turn back time and make it better.

So, we both went quiet and got on with preparing for Leaving exams and, for me, looking after the kids and, for

Jase, looking after his dad. Mr Price'd had a nasty accident in the grocery shop—fell off a ladder and busted his leg—so Jase was needed to help his Uncle Ken with lifting, carrying and unpacking boxes. Sometimes, Mum sent me down to Carey's Grocery and I'd see Jase stocking the shelves. We'd smile at each other and say hi, but that was about it. At school, we were just classmates and had our own friends. We rarely spoke.

Chapter Thirty

Christmas Holidays

Summer holidays felt empty without Em. There was no Christmas lebkuchen baking at Price's, no long walks together around the lake, no riding out to Rosie's farm, no plain hanging around together. Hers and Jase's birthday on January sixth came and went without any invitation to Price's for tea. Fair enough, I thought. Em wasn't there. Em was like a ghost in the Price's house. I wondered if they even mentioned her.

I spent some time around at the Larsen's. I hardly noticed Lily's scarring anymore. Somehow, it was just part of her and made her… her. 'Lovely Lily', Mum called her. I made sure to sit on her good side so she could hear me well. She attempted to teach me to spin, but I kept losing the wool into the bobbin and not being able to find the end again. I gave up and combed some wool for her. That I could do—the amount of practice I'd had doing my sisters' hair. I got to thinking about what I'd do when I left school. Did I really want to go to uni or teachers college? Did I need to stay at school? It still felt strange without Em. And I guess what happened to her made me a bit afraid of life beyond Yarralinga. Dad, who'd not got past Intermediate, had told me to finish my Matriculation. At least, then, I'd have more options.

Lily's voice broke my thoughts. 'Cuppa?' She stretched and arched her back. We chatted about Hans' next project over mugs of dandelion tea. I'd acquired a taste for it.

Some afternoons, when Mum didn't need me with the kids, I went with Gracie and Liz to the waterhole. Michael was home for a couple of weeks and came once. Gracie was beside herself, acting weird when he sauntered down the bank and said, 'Hi, ladies,' as he stripped to his shorts. He did look good. I heard Gracie suck in her breath. He stretched out next to her and talked to us about uni and looking forward to specialising in his subjects more in the coming year. Whatever that meant.

Gracie kept flicking her hair over her shoulder and nodding like a crested pigeon at what he said. He asked us about our own plans after school. Gracie said she was thinking about nursing, and when Michael told her that'd suit her, she blushed and said, 'Thanks!' as if he'd told her she was the most wonderful girl he'd ever met.

Oh, Gracie! I hoped she'd see he wasn't interested in her that way.

A cool change had come in during Friday night. No rain, but the skies were cloudy, so the sun wasn't frying us. Mum said it was high time for the older boys to help Dad in the garden and she wanted the girls to help with the house and little kids, so I could do what I wanted for the afternoon.

I took my library book and a yellow peach and went down to Crystal Lake to sit on the dam wall. Now, in late summer, it was low on water, its edges reedy and slimy. But I loved the smell and the quiet, broken only by a couple of late courting frogs.

I was just into the next chapter when Jase came along on his bike. He stopped by me. He had his racket and a bag of balls strapped to the carrier. He was wearing his tennis shoes, badly in need of whitening, and because I was sitting, his calves were in my line of sight. I could see little dark hairs over defined muscles. I couldn't look away.

'Hey, Jooles. Watcha reading?'

I cleared my throat, looked up at him and sort of squeaked, 'Hey, yourself.' I turned the cover toward him.

He read, '*My Love Must Wait*. Oh, soppy stuff.' And he pushed off for the tennis courts.

'It's not.' I found I was talking to myself, all the while following his tanned legs pumping the pedals. 'I wouldn't like to've been Matthew Flinders' wife. Waiting *years* for him to come home.'

I watched as he turned into the oval gates, calling to Tom Lawson who was already belting balls against the practice wall. The way Jase rode was so much like Em that a pain twanged in my chest. *God, make her be alright.*

DAD AND MUM finally convinced Lily and Hans to come around for morning tea one Saturday. Dad had sent Patrick, Sean and Conal off yabbying. We sat under the grapevine trellis by the back veranda while the girls and James and Aiden ran around in the sprinkler. Mum served scones with jam and cream, and mugs of Bushells tea. Lily had brought her own dandelion.

She was showing Mum and me the jumper she was knitting from wool she'd spun. It was for Hans to wear in his shed. 'He keeps working and doesn't realise how cold he's got,' she said. 'He comes inside freezing.'

'So, Hans,' said Dad. 'You're a bit of a dark horse, eh?'

Hans looked puzzled.

'Jooles was telling me about something she saw in the Art Gallery…?'

'Ah,' said Hans. He put the last bite of scone in his mouth and chewed slowly. He swallowed. 'Great scones, Fiona.' He wiped the cream off his moustache.

Dad said, 'Come on, mate. Can't get off that easily. Tell us. She said you've got sculptures everywhere.'

Hans laughed. 'Everywhere?' He looked at me.

I shrugged.

His eyes were dancing.

I thought of the dancing girl. 'It's Lily, isn't it. The girl in the Art Gallery.'

Hans nodded.

Lily spoke then. 'He carved it when we were at art school—final assignment. He said that one day I'd be able to dance like that again.' She was teary and smiling at once.

Hans reached out and took her hand. 'My biggest fan,' he said.

'He does have work in lots of places. I'm so very proud of what he's achieved. But I love that sculpture the best!'

Kathleen and Maria ran up, shiny wet and laughing and pulled Lily to her feet, and she became the dancing girl twirling through the sprinkler with them.

Chapter Thirty-One

Matriculation, 1972

The boy from Maud Springs was back when we started into Matriculation. I don't know how he put up with the bullying. At least when I was the focus, I had Gracie, Rosie and Liz. He had no friends. Candy and Co and some of the boys teased him mercilessly.

They called him Mawwwwd or Mawwwwdy. 'Hi, Mawwwwd!' 'Whatcha doin', Mawwwwdy?' Or sometimes 'Pimple Face' because he had a bad acne problem. I noticed the kids with acne never called him that.

His real name was Godfrey. He had a tapping habit— tap, tap, tap on the table with his pen or fingertips. Funny grunts, too. And when were we supposed to be motionless in assembly, he rocked from side to side, like mums do when they have hold of a pram or a baby. He just couldn't keep still. He hardly ever looked anyone in the face, even the teachers. He was different but super smart, too. He could answer Mr Donovan's maths problems while we were still finding our slide rules.

Candy flirted with him shamelessly, going uncomfortably close and murmuring stupid things like, 'Oh, God, free me! Free me, Godfreeee…' And in a wheedling voice, 'C'mon, Mawwwwdy. Ask me out. You know you want to…' Then she'd bump her hip against his. Poor kid would duck away with his head on his chest. He was always red-faced when she was around.

⁂

LATE IN MARCH, we were at the gates after school—Liz, Gracie and me—saying goodbye to Rosie who was getting on her bus. It drove away and the Murphy's car pulled into the spot it left.

Candy stomped over to the car, yanked the door open and let fly at her mum with unrepeatable names, something about why was her mum *so* late (which she wasn't). The milling kids stopped as if someone had called 'Freeze' in a game of statues. Sound ceased.

Until Candy slammed her door shut. We could still hear her ranting. Mrs Murphy blinkered and drove off. Fast.

Released from their frozen state, everyone gasped and 'woah-ed' and began to disperse, muttering, 'Unbelievable!' and 'No way!' as they went.

We were as stunned as everyone else.

Lizzy said, 'I'd never speak to my mum like that!'

'No. Dad'd never let us! Not that I'd want to, anyway.'

'Unbelievable!'

'Why's she like that?'

'I heard Mr Murphy swearing at Mrs Murphy once when I was walking past the pub,' said Gracie. 'Horrible man. Maybe Candy does it because he does.'

Murphys owned the Royal Hotel and Mrs Murphy was the housekeeper and cook.

I talked about it with Mum. 'Yes, I think Elizabeth is right,' she said. 'Mrs Murphy always looks worn out. Poor thing. She works so hard, but I don't think she gets much thanks for it.'

'Wouldn't say boo to a goose,' Dad added. 'Not that she goes out much for anyone to talk to her.'

When we told Mrs Friend about what we'd seen, she said, 'Can you think why Candice might be like that? What's happening for her that we don't know?'

I watched Candy a lot after that, trying to work out what was going on for her to make her so cruel. What was it like living in the pub? How did her mum and dad treat her? She always seemed 'full of herself' as Dad would say, but was that just for show? Underneath, what did she think of herself, really? I puzzled about it for a while, and then, May holidays came and I helped Mum with the house and kids. I didn't see Candy; I didn't think about her at all.

Early in Term 2, we had a visit from Mrs Price. She told us that Em had had the baby and she was alright. She would be at the Home for a little longer but then what would happen, she didn't know.

'I want her home, but Brian is still really angry. And ashamed. He just can't forgive her.'

'I'm sorry, Ruth.' Mum poured Mrs Price's tea and slid the milk and sugar toward her.

I had so many questions I wanted to ask but wasn't sure if I was allowed. Was it a girl or a boy? What did she call it? Where was it now? Did Em send her a letter and could I read it? I sat watching Mrs Price stir sugar into her tea in an absentminded way. Then she seemed to remember where she was and sighed. She tapped the spoon on the cup and placed it in the saucer.

'Thank you, Fiona. I'm grateful to have you. And Julie,' she added looking at me.

Mum said, 'No, we haven't said anything and we never will.'

'Thank you.'

Later that night, I could hear Mum and Dad talking in the sitting room. The walls of our house were a bit thin and my bed was right against the wall shared with the sitting room. Mum was asking Dad to talk to Mr Price to convince him to bring his daughter home. 'You'd want to, Barry, if it was Julie.' I heard Dad mumble assent and then some rustling and giggling and then footsteps. Their bedroom door clicked shut. Ah, parents! I was glad their room was on the other side of the house.

Dad talked to Mr Price. He went over with a bucket of beetroot, carrots and half a dozen beers one Friday after work. He didn't come home until we'd eaten our fish and his was keeping hot under a saucepan lid on the side of the stove. The kids were either in the bath or in their rooms.

'Well?' asked Mum.

'Done,' said Dad.

Mum wasn't satisfied. 'And?'

'That's it. He'll let her come home.'

Mum clapped her hands and hugged him. 'That's wonderful!'

I made it a group hug. 'Thanks, Dad. Thanks!'

Mum asked, 'How did you convince him, Barry?'

Dad tapped the side of his nose. 'Men's business, Fi. Secret men's business.'

Chapter Thirty-Two

I stopped beside the noticeboard out front of Carey's Grocery to see who'd lost a dog or found one, who was picked for footy and netball that Saturday, what things people had put up for sale...

Large, pink, glittery letters on a purple background caught my eye—Debutante Ball. Smaller text stated that if you were in Leaving or Matriculation and were interested in being part of a Debutante Ball to be held in September, you should contact Mrs Bloomingdale.

I mentioned it to Mum that night when we were washing up. Her eyes lit up. 'Yes, I was going to ask if you wanted to be part of it.'

'I dunno, Mum. I mean, it's a bit old fashioned, isn't it? Like "Here they are, guys. Come and get 'em!"'

Mum laughed. 'You make it sound like it's open slather, no restraint from now on. Yes, it is old-fashioned and Yarralinga's certainly not Victorian high society, but they are a lot of fun. And we'd be raising money for a new roof for the Institute.' (Did I say Mum was on the Institute committee, too? Of course).

'Did you do your deb?' I asked.

'Oh, yes,' breathed Mum, her eyes all sparkly again. 'Dad was my partner. That was the time that clinched it for us.'

I watched her go soft and gooey as she remembered, and wondered if I would have a story like that someday.

So, who would partner me? I mean, the rumours that Justin started had seeped down deep into a lot of guys' minds. I found them watching sometimes when I talked with other girls, as if they expected me to kiss one of them there and then. It creeped me out.

Mum suggested I ask Jason. 'You get on well and you've grown up together. Be different if Em was here. He'd probably accompany her, then. But she isn't, so…'

'I dunno, Mum. We hardly talk much anymore, not since…'

'Not since what?'

'You know, since Justin Waters said that stuff about me and Em.'

'Oh, Julie. That was ages ago. In Intermediate, I think? Surely people don't believe that!'

'Yeah, well, guys avoid me like the plague. I don't think I'll do it. Look silly if I have to come down the steps by myself.'

Mum turned from the washing up, dried her hands on her apron and placed them on my shoulders. She looked in my eyes. Uh, oh, this was going to be her final decision.

'Julie, Jason Price is a good boy. I'm sure he can tell what is truth and what is not. Give him some credit.' She dropped her hands. 'Ask him to be your partner. Or I will.'

So, I did. I timed it so he was following me down Wattle Street after school. I made to do a cool turn and stop at Murray to wait for him. But my front wheel hit loose gravel that the council had tried to patch a pothole with. I slid sideways and landed with the bike between my legs and my bag smashed under the back wheel. *Elegant, Jooles, so elegant! Mortifying!*

I heard Jase stop beside me. 'You alright, Jooles?'

At least, I got his attention. 'Yeah, yeah, all good,' I said as I tried to extricate myself. But instead of the coordinated jump to my feet that I envisaged, my foot got tangled in the forks and I went bum up over the handlebars (thank God for pantyhose!) smack into Jase's bike, bringing him down with me. We lay there. Stunned. Speechless.

Then he laughed, that awesome belly laugh like Em's, and I realised that his voice had deepened. *When did that happen?* How could I not laugh too, even though my knee was shooting with pain like a thousand mozzies stinging at once.

Other kids were around us then, pointing and laughing.

'What happened? You alright?' It was Gracie reaching out her hand to me.

But Jase got there first. He was on his feet and lifting me by the hand.

'Ah! My knee!' I sucked in my breath as I put weight on

my leg. It wouldn't hold. I slumped against him and slid down his side onto the ground. He sat down next to me and felt my already swelling knee.

'Not good,' he said.

'Listen, I'll go get your mum to come with the car,' said Gracie and rode off up Murray Street.

The other kids lost interest then. Who needs to hang around and see a big matric kid wait for her mum? Only Jase stayed. And that's when I asked him to partner me for the Deb Ball.

'Only if you want to, I mean. You don't have to.' *Come on, Jooles. Get a grip!* 'I mean, maybe Em wants you to partner her. Or has someone else asked you? Oh, sorry, that's none of my business…' *Oh, for goodness' sake!*

Jase had this strange look on his face. Like Em when I said I was going to church. They were so much alike, those two. He was looking at me sideways with his fringe falling part into his eyes. His lovely brown eyes. My stomach was doing flip-flops. Probably 'cos I'd just fallen over. My face was hot, too.

'You're funny, Jooles Kent.' *Really? Funny? I just made total hash of asking you to partner me and you tell me I'm funny? Well, yeah, a little bit, I guess.* I stifled a giggle, but it still slipped out.

Jase said, 'Em doesn't want to ever do her deb. Says it's "a pointless waste of time". Unquote.'

And so…? I realised I was holding my breath. *Better breathe before I pass out against him…*

'Yeah, I'll partner you, Jooles. It'll be fun.'

'You will?' I saw he wasn't pulling my leg (even though

he still had his hand on my knee) 'Oh, you will. Great. Thank you.' *Fun. Funny. Lots of fun. Yep, it will be sooo much fun! Yoikes, girl, you gotta think of some other words!*

We sat there, side by side in silence. I didn't have the heart to ask Jase to remove his hand, even though my knee was throbbing and blown up twice the size of the other one. I was a bit disappointed when Mum pulled up next to us and fussed, helping me into the car. It meant that Jase was left to load my bike into the boot.

'Thank you for looking after her, Jason,' smiled Mum.

'You're welcome, Mrs Kent. Anytime.'

Anytime? Whoa!

SEEING each other wasn't awkward after that and we saw each other lots. Besides school, I mean. That didn't count much because we each had our own set of friends and those of us sitting our Matriculation had heads down in study. It was at the practices for the Deb Ball that we hung out most and with the other couples—Gracie and Tom Lawson (she wanted to ask Michael, but he was off at uni), Liz and her brother Geoff, Suzy and Brian Williams, Candy and Justin (yes, she finally got to be with him), Rosie and her brother Connor, Lorrie Schwartz and Peter May, and six younger couples from Leaving.

My knee got better quickly. Thankfully. After my invitation to Jase being accepted, I wasn't going to sit on the sidelines while someone else accompanied him.

Mrs Bloomingdale coached us in the finer points of the

Queen's Waltz and—'if you would only behave yourselves,' she said in an exasperated voice—of the Military Two. But it was the one night a week we gave ourselves off studying, and so the air was charged. We were charged.

Chapter Thirty-Three

Nina McCarthy, Rosie's aunt, 'rough as bags but with a heart of gold' according to Dad, was stylist for occasions like weddings—teasing and winding and spraying hair into intricate, sleek dos, when her own hair was never like that. 'No time,' she said, and so she wore it pulled into a messy ponytail wound about with a fluffy band that probably belonged to one of her girls. Blonde-white strands fell out around her face, but she never seemed to notice as she concentrated on the client's hair in her hands.

I was in awe. I'd never been to a hairdresser before. Mum always trimmed our hair. A hairdresser was the one concession Dad and Mum had made to spending money on the Deb Ball.

My dress had been made by Granny Murphy (yeah, I know, also Candy's surname: somewhere way back, our family tree branches got tangled so we're some sort of cousins, hopefully lots and *lots* removed) from fabric that

Mum had picked up in a sale years ago—a heavy white damask. I suspected that it was curtaining but hated to ask. At least it covered my shoes that had once been brown but now were painted white. 'They'll have to do,' said Mum. 'Can't quite afford a new pair at the moment.' Still, if it was a choice between a hairdo and new shoes, well, it was no choice really.

So here I was sitting in Swanton's Hair Salon, swathed in a pink cape, staring at my reflection in the mirror while Nina fussed around preparing her trolley. Gracie, Rosie and Liz hovered, and scanned the magazines for ideas for their own styles.

'Well, girls,' said Nina, 'this is a bit like getting ready for a wedding, ain't it? The bride and her maids. Sure that's not what this is all about?'

We giggled.

'One day, eh? Just take your time and find the right guy. One that really looks out for you.'

She was quiet for a while, concentrating on curling a length of hair around her fingers, spraying it and pinning it to my head. 'Don't do what I did, eh? Fall for the first guy to take a shine. Stupid mistake. Takes a while to get past the past, you know.' The air was thick with spray and something about to be revealed. Nina placed the can on the trolley, put her hands on her hips and surveyed us all.

'I got two parts to my life. I call them BC, Before Christ, and WC, With Christ, though that's not quite right really 'cos BC was the shitty part.' And she guffawed openly.

I glanced wide-eyed at the others in the mirror. I could see they were feeling a bit embarrassed by her language, too, but we giggled anyway.

'And it's 'cos I didn't think enough of me to wait for someone who did.'

Of course, everyone knew her story and applauded how she'd changed her life around. 'I had a lot of help from my family and the church.' She was fond of repeating this fact. 'If not for all of them, dunno what would've become of me. Or my girls.' She shuddered. 'They're the only good thing to come out of that time.'

I watched Nina as she worked, puzzled as to why she looked different in the mirror than face-to-face. Then I realised it was her nose. It was bent to one side, making her reflection look odd. Nina noticed me studying it. 'BC war wound,' she said, tapping her nose with her styling comb. 'I repeat, take your time to find one who *really* cares for you.'

I thought about that a lot while Nina worked her magic on my mousy hair, on Liz's straight chestnut, Rosie's wavy blonde and Gracie's curly red (I envied that hair even though she hated it). I thought about Mum and Dad. They were the first and only for each other yet, look! Their marriage was going strong, and they were still good to each other even with a tribe of nine kids. Yeah, nine looked like that was it. 'Let's not go cheaper by the dozen, eh, love?' I overheard Mum say to Dad late one night.

I thought about my grandparents. Both sets had celebrated their fortieth wedding anniversaries, and you don't do that many years with someone unkind. Do you?

Then I thought of Jase and dancing with him, maybe even *kissing* him, and my stomach flip-flopped. I looked down close at the magazine, wishing my hair would fall over my hot face. But Nina had used a whole can of spray and a tin of bobby pins on it. It wasn't going anywhere.

Was that how you could tell? When your stomach somersaulted, and your face went hot? I looked at Nina. She must've felt like that, otherwise she wouldn't have gone with those guys, married them. Would she? So how could you tell who was the right one? How did you know you were in love, and it was for keeps, for ever and ever till death do you part?

When Nina finally ushered us out the door, her parting words stuck with me. 'You girls make sure that tonight's not the only time you qualify to wear white. Wait for the *right* one. And the *right* time.'

Chapter Thirty-Four

'Thanks for being fine with the dress, Julie,' said Mum in short-of-breath way as if she was nervous. She finished sliding the zip up my back and then smoothed her hands across my shoulders. 'I promise that when you get married, you can choose whatever you want for your wedding dress.'

'Oh, Mum, it's all good. It fits well, doesn't it?' We gazed at our reflections in her cheval mirror. Granny Murphy really had done herself proud with my dress. It was a simple empire-line with a scooped neck trimmed with beads, and short sleeves, also trimmed with beads, that folded over on themselves like rose petals. Not bad for curtain material.

'Yes, it does. Julie, you look beautiful.' She had shiny eyes. 'Well, off you go, and I'll just finish getting myself ready. Won't be long.'

When I walked into the kitchen, Dad gave out a low whistle. I blushed.

'Wow, girlie!' he said, and a smile lit his face. He clapped his hands together and made to come in for a hug, but then changed his mind as if afraid to mess up my dress or something.

So, I opened my arms. 'Thanks, Dad.'

He held me then in such a tight squeeze, I'm not sure if it was that that made tears pop out or if it was his reaction to seeing me dressed for the ball. He let me go. I patted under my eyes hoping there were no mascara smudges.

Then he offered his hand and said, 'May I have the first dance, young lady?' He scooped me into his frame and waltzed me around the table humming *La Paloma* as we went.

The kids came tumbling in after Gramma Kent, there to babysit. The boys were dressed as if for church with their hair Brylcreemed in place. The girls giggled to see us dancing.

Then Patrick said, 'Dah-dah-da-daaaah!' as Mum made her entrance. Dad dropped his arms and wolf whistled shrilly. Kathleen yelped and put her hands over her ears. Maria's eyes were the size of saucers. Sean and Conal laughed loudly. It was a good thing the twins and Brigid were already asleep, or we would've been late while Mum settled them again.

'And who is this fabulous-looking woman?' asked Dad. ''Scuse me,' he said, bowing to me. 'I've *gotta* introduce meself.'

He was right. Mum did look fabulous. Even after birthing nine kids and raising us this far, she was still slim and curvy in all the right places. She was wearing her swirling, midnight-blue taffeta gown (she'd worn it to dances every year since I could remember) with her pearl earrings and matching necklace (a wedding present from her parents) and had swept her hair into a neat chignon (the only up-style she could manage herself). Granny Murphy's fur wrap was draped around her shoulders. She looked like a princess. No, a queen. Regal.

'Come dance with me, beautiful lady,' sang Dad as he swept her into his embrace and waltzed off around the table again with us kids sidestepping or leaping onto the chairs to make room. I got backed into the pantry doorway as Mum's dress swished past. Maria and Kathleen were so overcome to see Mum and Dad so lovey-dovey, they were hugging each other and jumping up and down, giggling, sparkly-eyed. I saw blushes and sparkly eyes on the boys, too. When Mum and Dad came around again, the girls lifted their arms. 'Me, too! Me! I wanna dance!' So, Mum and Dad picked up one each and continued around the table. Good job they were still tiny for their age.

I kept checking the kitchen clock. This was good: it was better than good to see my parents so happy. But I didn't want to be late. I plucked Dad's arm as he waltzed past. 'Dad! Can we go? Please?'

I saw him glance at the clock. 'Oh, yeah, righto,' he said. He placed Maria on the floor and kissed the back of her hand. 'You are a lovely dancer, Miss Maria Kent.' She attempted a thank you curtsy like she'd seen me practise but got muddled in her nightie and fell on her bottom. Dad scooped her up again, snuggled her out of her embarrassment then passed her over to Gramma Kent.

'Right, boys. You know the drill. Don't go sneaking off.

It's straight home after the first set of dances and obey your Gramma.'

'I want a full description of every dress and dance, thank you very much,' ordered Gramma.

'Yes, Gramma,' said the boys in unison.

That'll be the day!

Dad offered Mum and me an arm each. We hooked in, but of course we were too wide for the door and the hallway, so I had to let go and follow with the boys. Oh, well, it's the thought that counts.

'Bye,' called Gramma. 'Have a lovely time!'

We came out into a half-moonlit night. Crispy air like it might be a late frost. I pulled the knitted shawl (Granny Murphy's) close around me. Behind us, Gramma called, 'I'll keep the front light on for you.'

The light bounced across the front yard. Jase was standing by his dad's car at the gate, looking at me. He gave a soft whistle. *Flip-flop! Red-hot! Wow, he looks so good in a suit.* I let the shawl slip to my elbows.

Mum and Dad stopped as Jase came toward us. I came up beside Dad and smiled at Jase. *Oh, so good!*

'Hullo, hullo,' said Dad, more loudly than necessary.

I glanced at Dad and saw he was feigning surprise. Mum was trying not to smile, but her glowing face was a dead give-away.

'And what can we do for you, young fella?'

I was never prouder of Jase than at that moment when he showed he knew my dad was having a go. He drew himself tall, stepped forward and said loudly (but not as loudly as Dad), 'Mr Kent, sir, may I please accompany your daughter to the Debutante Ball?'

Quick as a wink, Dad shot back, 'Ah, but I have four, young man, and none of them of marriageable age.'

'Ow!' he added as Mum poked him in the side.

Dad! This is only a Deb Ball!

Jase flicked his eyes to me. I tried to will him on, but how do you do that with only a look? *Don't back down, Jase. You can do it.*

Jase looked back to Dad. 'Then, I'll wait. Sir.' *Flip-flop. And shivery knees!*

That stopped Dad for six ordinary heartbeats (not mine, 'cos it was pounding out of my chest like a galloping horse) before he said, 'Well, it'll be a long time, lad. Brigid is still in nappies. Maria, she's only…' Here he faltered. He couldn't remember.

'Eight,' whispered Mum.

'Eight. And Kathleen, she's only…'

'Six.'

Dad was fast winding down. 'Six. Humpff… so… yeah, alright, you win!' and he was done. He let go a huge belly laugh as he grabbed Jase's hand and pumped it up and down. Then he took my hand and placed it in Jase's. 'Look after her, son!' he said, beetling his eyebrows. 'Don't let her trip down them steps.'

'Yes, sir!' said Jase.

Oh, heck, don't salute and click your heels as well!

But he didn't. Even though he'd beaten Dad fair and square at his own game, he knew when to stop.

Dad placed Mum's hand on his arm and strode off down the path and out the gate to our car.

The boys looked like they were still trying to catch on and stared at Jase and me before racing after them.

Behind us, I heard Gramma say, 'Gotcha! Smart alec,' and laugh softly as she shut the door.

I wanted to leap on Jase then and there and kiss him right on those open, smiling lips. But I didn't. I mean, we were dressed up, and it was getting late, and we had somewhere to go and *oh, he's leaning in close, his hands are warm on my bare arms, he smells so good, he's going to kiss me… flip-flop!*

Chapter Thirty-Five

We rushed into the supper rooms that doubled as change rooms for concerts. Last. All eyes turned to us, and I know I blushed deeply. *They can tell. I'm sure they can tell we kissed.* Jase dropped my hand to take my corsage from Mrs Bloomingdale.

But she held it fast. 'I will pin it, thank you, Jason. You may join the other boys.' He was dismissed. He winked at me from behind her—I had to stifle a giggle—as Mrs Bloomingdale pinned the corsage to my shoulder and a recalcitrant strand of hair to my head (always prepared with bobby pins, safety pins and tissues). She wiped the corner of my mouth. Had kissing smudged my lipstick? *Oh, heck!*

'You look lovely, my dear.' Off went Mrs Bloomingdale to check that everything was ready.

Jase had wandered over to the guys. Gracie, Liz, Rosie and the rest of the girls pounced on me. Gracie took my arm and turned me one-eighty. She looked gorgeous in a cream empire-line with a sweetheart neckline and puff sleeves. She handed me a compact and a lippy from her reticule. And nodded.

'Thanks,' I whispered, blushing as I saw what kissing had done to my careful application. 'Thanks,' I whispered again as I handed them back.

'All good.' She grinned. 'Tell me about it later, yeah?'

We joined the others, admiring their dresses and dos, pretending to like those we didn't for the sake of peace. We didn't have to pretend with Liz's though. It had belonged to her great-aunt Tabby, back in the twenties—no sleeves, v-neckline, a long, beaded bodice over a lacy skirt.

'Wow! Your aunty was such an amazing dressmaker!'

'Stunning!'

'Thanks.' She beamed and held out the skirt as she swished from side to side.

Suze had designed and made her own dress—she so should go into fashion design after school. It fitted snug to her body and flowed into a wide skirt that spun out as she twirled to show us.

'Wow! You are an amazing dressmaker, Suze!'

She glowed.

Candy's was dramatic, of course, clingy and showing more cleavage than was modest, something that Mrs Bloomingdale had expressly warned us not to do. *Justin'll love that!* And she'd done racoon eyes with eyeliner, something that the photographer had expressly warned us not to do.

Mrs Bloomingdale clapped her hands loudly and called, 'Places everyone. NOW, I know what they say in show business but do NOT break a leg at my Debutante Ball!

Remember, boys, to hand your girls down those steps safely.'

Jase came close again. 'I have to tell you something. It's Em. She's here.'

I scanned the room. 'What, now?' before I realised he meant out in the hall. 'Aren't debs a "pointless waste of time" unquote?'

'Well, she is and said she hopes you'll talk to her.'

'What? Why wouldn't I talk to her? Can't wait to see her. It's been *ages*.'

'Great.' He leaned in. *Not here Jase. Not in front of every-one!* 'See you soon, Jooles,' he said softly about an inch from my ear. How was I ever going to walk down those steps with wibbly-wobbly knees?

There was something in the way Candy sang beneath her breath as she slid past me, 'Ooo, Julie's got a boyfriend,' that made my shoulder blades creep. *Watch out, Jase. Candy's jealous.*

We girls pulled on our gloves and took turns to peer into the hall through a gap in the stage curtains. It looked like all Yarralinga had come. I spotted Michael Boston near the front. He looked good. Uni suited him. There was a girl standing next to him and she was smiling up at him, at something he'd said. She had her hand on his arm. I looked at Gracie. She'd seen, too. She was chewing her bottom lip like it was a piece of gristle. *Don't cry, Gracie. Your mascara'll run.* I reached out and touched her shoulder. She looked at me and nodded.

'I'm alright,' she said. Pretty unconvincing voice, but she was trying, so I didn't reply.

One by one, we were to stand under an arch of flowers

and watch as the girl in front of us did her walk across the middle of the stage to meet her partner at the top of the steps. Then he offered his hand and walked backward down the steps, steadying her as she kept her eyes ahead. All very well to warn the girls about broken legs but what about the guys walking backwards?

I was third in line, so I used my time under the arch to scan the room for Em. I couldn't see her. Too many people pressed together, and the back of the hall was in semi-darkness. Every now and then, light reflected off someone's glasses as they craned their necks to get a better view.

Candy was ahead of me. She was already tall but was wearing really high, skinny heels (something else that Mrs Bloomingdale had warned us not to do) that put an extra ten centimetres on her height... or maybe only seven... I don't know, but really tall... and made Justin (well-built, remember?) look like a weed alongside her. She got to the top of the stairs in a sort of teetering hobble and paused for him to meet her.

They were nearly to the bottom when she stumbled— maybe her shoe caught a snag in the carpet—and fell toward him. His reaction time was impeccable but where he grabbed her was not. The crowd gasped as his left hand clutched her arm and his right hand her boob. *Yep, very manly, Justin, very manly. And I have to follow that?* How she didn't even flinch or biff him or cry out or anything, I don't know. She just calmly unhooked his hands, linked her arm into his and led him down toward the twinkling-eyed Mayor and his trying-to-maintain-a-poker-face wife.

'May I present Miss Candy Murphy accompanied by Mr Justin Waters,' intoned Mrs Bloomingdale. *Did she even see* what just happened? I mean how can she be so serious when everyone else is dying to laugh out loud?

Then it was my turn. My legs were shaking. Like a lamb to slaughter. Everyone's watching me… I wobbled a bit, coming down off the platform, but then, Jase was at the top of the steps holding out his hand, and I couldn't help but return his grin and lock onto those gorgeous eyes. S'posed to look at the Mayor, Jooles. No, I can't. I'm under a spell. Sheesh, girl, get a grip! His eyes held mine until we reached the bottom of the steps and we turned to walk the carpet.

'May I present Miss Julie Kent accompanied by Mr Jason Price,' intoned Mrs Bloomingdale.

Look at the Mayor and his wife. Smile. Don't do a Maria curtsy. Right step, left step, right behind, bend knees and up. Alright! All good. Shake hands. Breathe…

As we turned away to take our places in the circle, I spotted Em at the back of the crowd. It was hard to see her properly. I only just stopped myself from waving and calling to her.

When everyone had been presented—thirteen debutantes and their partners—we danced the Queen's Waltz while the crowd smiled upon us. My legs felt as unyielding as wooden garden stakes. They just wouldn't bend at the knees.

'Relax,' said Jase softly into my hair as he turned me into the waltz part.

Mum said Dad was a natural dancer. He's got the music in him. That's Jase, too. And so, I focused on his right ear and felt his left hand at the small of my back guiding me. Warm. Safe. The music finished. Already?

The crowd cheered and clapped us, and Mr Knight

invited everyone else to the dance floor. Dad was at my side. 'Thanks, son, you did a great job,' he said to Jase, 'Now, my turn to dance with my daughter,' and grabbed my hand.

Jase nodded his head. Once. 'Yes sir, Mr Kent.'

The band launched into the Military Two-Step and away we went, following the other couples through the sawdust. I kept scanning the room for Em in the first steps where I wasn't looking into Dad's shoulder (he's a lot taller than me). I couldn't see her anywhere. I lost sight of Jase, too, but as soon as the dance finished, he was there being cheeky to Dad.

'Now, my turn to dance with your daughter. Please, sir.'

Dad spluttered a bit and said, 'I'm off to find an older woman then.'

I heard him chuckle as he walked away to Mum. I turned to Jase. He was grinning. I felt warm all over like when I got picked first for the skipping team and the other captain groaned because she wanted me. I grinned back. Then I remembered.

'I saw Em,' I said. 'Now, I can't.'

'Yeah. She went,' said Jase. 'When you were dancing with your dad. She didn't really want to be here. Just to see us presented. Come over tomorrow, yeah?'

'Yeah, yeah, I will.' I beamed. I wasn't sure if the little jolt in my tummy was because Jase was asking me or if I'd get to see Em *and* Jase. Maybe both. *Yeah, definitely both!*

Chapter Thirty-Six

Dad found Patrick, Sean and Conal skulking around the drinks table and hauled them back home to Gramma. 'Don't forget to give her every detail,' he told them sternly.

'Yes,' Gramma would tell him when he quizzed her later, 'they told me about every dress. White. White. White. And long. Very informative. Oh, and Patrick said that Candy Murphy was very pretty.'

Mrs Price played the piano. I think she liked to hide there rather than join the talk and dancing and being among the crowd. She was so shy. But Mr Price got Mr Lawson to play for one song so he could dance with her. I was surprised at how well she could.

Mum was in her element, chatting to other ladies and accepting dances with every man who asked her. Until Dad got back from taking the boys home, and then he steered her onto the dance floor as soon as Mr Knight announced,

'Gentlemen, take your partners…' They looked so good together. So happy. So young.

Sure enough, Justin couldn't keep his eyes off Candy's cleavage after their entrance. I thought for a moment he was going to grab her again. But she got away from him after the Pride of Erin and bailed up Jase between the drinks table and the supper-room stairs. She shot out her hand and grabbed the fruit punch he was bringing back for me.

'Thanks, Jason. You're a sweetheart. I'm so thirsty.' She downed the lot and licked her lips slowly, all the while staring into his eyes, his eyes that were wide with surprise and consternation. She moved closer in her towering heels. That brought her boobs right in front of Jase's chin. He was struggling to keep looking up, I could tell.

Right, that's it! I went for her. Yeah, well, so not like I'd envisaged in my mind.

I came up behind her and, reaching up on tiptoes, I put my hand beside my mouth to whisper in her ear. She gulped, turned so her back was to the wall, and her hands shot to the back of her dress to twitch it back and forth.

'Come on, Jase,' I said. 'Let's dance.'

Jase was laughing as we walked away. 'What did you say to her?'

I put on my serious face. 'Oh, just that her dress was stuck up you know where. That's what happens with clingy jersey.'

He laughed loud then and scooped me into his arms for the foxtrot. I glanced back to see Candy sidling out toward the toilets with a face the colour of ripe tomatoes.

While the ladies laid the supper out, Dad helped Mr Swanton scatter more sawdust on the floor. A couple of little kids were running and skidding in it. Mrs Bloomingdale marched across and told them off and they shot back to their totally unaware mums who were nattering by the stage. The kids slid under their mother's chairs and hid.

I saw Candy's mum sitting in a corner. Nobody seemed to be talking to her and Candy's dad was off at the bar laughing and talking loudly with some other men, Mr Hawkins and Mr Vincent among them. I didn't see him dance with Candy's mum even once. Later, after supper, she fussed around clearing plates and escaped to the kitchens.

We were standing at the supper table, Jase and me, Gracie and Tom, and Liz and Rosie (their brothers had gone off with their friends, having done their duty accompanying their sisters). Mrs Hawkins and Mrs Vincent were sitting against the wall behind us, making comments to each other about the dancers. Rev and Mrs Friend danced past.

Mrs Hawkins said, 'Mutton dressed as lamb, that one!'

I watched as Rev and Mrs Friend turned through a waltz, her full, floaty skirt spinning out, like a lemon butterfly, and thought she looked stunning. His hand wasn't on her lower back like Mrs Bloomingdale had taught the boys, but higher, on her bare skin—her dress was a halter neck. I felt a shivery tingle between my own shoulder blades.

I glared back at Mrs Hawkins—wearing her ancient, dowdy fox fur, its black, beady eyes looking just like her own—but she didn't notice me. Mrs Vincent did and looked away from her friend as her face went pale.

 I turned back to my friends.

Tom was talking about how he'd killed a brown snake in their backyard when 'Oh!' slipped out of Gracie's mouth and she turned towards the table. I didn't think she really wanted another fairy cake so I turned to where she'd been looking.

Michael Boston and his girlfriend stood there next to Rosie. 'Hi,' he said.

We all chimed 'Hi' back, but then this awkward silence followed. I poked Gracie in the arm, and she slowly turned back and mumbled 'Hi' through a mouthful of cake. There was a bit of cream just above her top lip. It looked like a zit. I tapped my own lip until she cottoned on and wiped it away.

'Umm, great to see you all,' said Michael. 'Really great!'

Got anything else? Like who's your friend?

Did she hear me? Because, next thing, she poked him in the arm. He coloured and coughed and said, 'Oh, yeah, this is Cilla. Umm, this is… everyone.'

Really? That's all you got? I wanted to biff him. *What've you done with our Michael?*

Cilla raised her palm and gave a sort of curly-fingered wave, 'Good to meet you all,' she gushed. 'Mikey talks about you *all* the time.'

Mikey? Who's Mikey. It's Michael, you airhead!

'Lots of good stuff,' she added. 'Do they only do this kind of dancing? When's the fun dancing start? You know…' She lifted her arms and swung her hips around, singing the chorus of *Everlasting Love* like she was on the dance floor with only Michael. She looked in his eyes the whole time.

Gag! I wanna gag! I glanced at Gracie. Her face mirrored everyone else's—ogle-eyed.

Right then, Mr Knight tapped the microphone and called, 'Gentlemen, take your partners for the Modern Waltz.' Gracie sort of shook herself and turned to Tom. 'Yes, Tom, I'd love to,' she said before he even asked, and steered him away. Michael's eyes followed her.

Yeah, doesn't she look gorgeous, you idiot.

Then Cilla said, 'Ooh, modern, huh? Like, slow dancing? Come on, Mikey.' He gulped and a muscle in his jaw twitched as she pulled him out onto the sawdust.

Later, Jase led me out to start in the progressive Canadian Barn Dance. I wasn't keen on that dance and kept looking to see how many men to go before I got around to him again. The men said things like, 'Aren't you Barry Kent's daughter?' 'My, you've grown up.' 'I danced with your mother. Delightful!' The music stopped before I got back to Jase, but he came straight to me and wove his fingers into mine. We stood there side-by-side, my fingers tingly and me wondering what he was thinking.

Mr Swanton announced that he'd like the men and boys to all pitch in and help with clean up—things like sweeping the floor and stacking the supper tables away. That done, everyone collected their wraps and furs and handbags, and headed for the door.

'Alright,' said Dad to Jase and me. 'See you at home. Soon. *Real* soon!'

'Yes sir,' said Jase.

Mum leaned in and kissed my cheek. She smelled of

Midnight in Paris perfume, and I wondered what that would be like—midnight in Paris.

'See you at home soon, love.'

And they were gone.

Jase held the car door open for me to slide in.

Chapter Thirty-Seven

When I came home, the house was still. Sleeping. Or so I thought. But I'd just got a glass of water from the kitchen tap when Mum appeared. She was wearing her mauve chenille dressing gown and fluffy slippers, and her hair was tumbling around her shoulders. I loved that she kept her hair long when so many ladies her age had it cut short and permed. She looked pink and pretty and, although sleepy, her eyes sparkled.

'Hullo, love,' she said. 'I wondered if you wanted help to get the bobby pins out.'

I smiled and nodded. 'Thanks.' We both knew that, really, she wanted to talk.

I sat at the table, and she began to undo Nina's work. Every pin out was a release. I hadn't realised how much my head was hurting.

'You looked very beautiful tonight, my love,' said Mum. She rested her hands on my shoulders and leaned down to kiss my cheek. 'I feel very proud of you. We both do.'

I felt a warmth like thick honey fill my belly. 'Thanks, Mum.'

She went on pulling pins. 'Did you have a good time?'

I could tell from her voice that she was smiling. 'Yes. Yes, it was the best. Thanks for everything.'

'I'm glad. There that's the last of them.' She combed her fingers through my hair. 'Give it a good brushing before bed. To get the hairspray out. Now, a cup of Milo?'

Even though I just wanted to go to bed and relive the night as I went to sleep, I nodded. And I did want to tell Mum about Jase and me. A little bit, anyway. So, we sat together, and it felt like I was talking to Em. Maybe Mum was my best friend, too. She held my hands and looked in my eyes, and there was a soft sheen in hers when I told her I really liked Jase. A lot. And that we kissed. I felt hot when I said that, and I looked down. She just squeezed my hands and waited for me to say more.

When I didn't, she said, 'He's a good boy, Julie. But look after yourself when you are with him, won't you? Do you know what I mean?'

Then I remembered her saying, when she told me Em was pregnant, 'It can happen to good girls, too.' And now I thought I knew what she meant—how the shivery thrills I felt when I kissed Jase could take over. I supposed good boys could go too far, too.

I nodded.

LATE NEXT MORNING, I walked over to the Price's with my

hair feeling free of the bobby pins and hairspray, but with my stomach flip-flopping at the thought of seeing Jase.

Oma wasn't sitting on the veranda. It was far too cold and cloudy. Even the dog wasn't in his favourite spot. Usually, I would have called 'Hullo' and gone inside, but this morning the door was closed against the bitter breeze. I knocked. The door sprang open and there was Jase, beaming like the sun that should have been shining.

He pulled me into the hallway and planted a kiss on my lips before I could say, 'Hi!' Then he let go and said, 'Em's in her room. I just had to get in first.' He grinned.

I giggled like Kathleen had that morning when she found two cents under her pillow instead of the tooth she'd put there. My stomach settled, and I went in for another sweet kiss. Then I pushed him away and sang, 'Later,' and skipped down to Em's door.

I hadn't seen her since, when? Felt like forever. She stood with the door half-open, gazing at me with brown eyes that seemed too big for her thin, pale face. She'd cropped her hair short and dyed it even darker. Black, I think. I paused.

'Hi, Em.'

She nodded and opened the door fully, but instead of moving to hug me, she turned and went to sit cross-legged on her bed. She was wearing old, corded jeans and the baggy knitted jumper she used to wear to footy.

'Wanna go for a walk?' I asked. 'I know it's cold but be good to.'

I could tell she wanted to stay in her room, warm and safe, but she slowly nodded and got up. She fished her shoes out from under the bed and pulled a scarf and beanie from the peg behind the door.

I was glad Jase was nowhere to be seen when we left. I needed this time with Em by herself. We didn't say anything all the way past the school and over the main road. It was freezing, a lazy wind not bothering to go around us. I stuffed my hands into my coat pockets and wished I'd worn my beanie.

We walked in awkward silence. Who was this person next to me? She walked with her head bent and her scarf pulled up over her lower face so that just her downcast eyes showed between it and her beanie. Her shoulders were slumped forward and she had stuffed her hands into her sleeves—for more reason than being cold. Where was my bouncy, full-of-life friend?

We sat on the dam wall and dangled our legs over the side. Even though it was June, there was hardly any more water than in January. Farmers were still hoping and praying for good winter rains.

Suddenly, Em said, 'I'm not going back to that school. I've missed so much, and I just can't face them anymore. Aunty Sue and Uncle Steve are pretty mad at me and Larry. And so's Dad. He won't even talk to me. It's weird, but Mum's different. She says I should come back home and finish here. But I dunno. They made us keep up with our studies in the Home, but I think I'll be miles behind.'

'Come home, Em, please. What else would you do? Change schools? Get a job?'

Em shrugged. 'I dunno.' She turned to face me. Suddenly, I saw the old Em, the one who stood up to Justin for me, the one who fought back against what she thought was wrong. Her voice was sharp as knives. 'It wouldn't be the same though, would it? You've got the other girls to hang around with now. You never even wrote to me once when I was in the Home! You don't really care.' And she turned away to throw a rock into the dam. It hit the surface hard, sending spray high into the air. Two ducks took fright and flew off squawking.

My mouth hung open. My throat burned. I felt cut. I stared at the water settling as the ripples petered out. *What about the letters I sent you after Mum and I came to town to see you? You never replied to those!*

'But I wasn't allowed to,' I said.

Em's voice was flat as if she'd used all her energy in that one outburst. 'Allowed to what?'

'To write to you at the Home. Mum said that your mum said I couldn't.' I was crying now. 'I wanted to, Em. I missed you so much, but I wasn't allowed. I thought it was the rules of the Home.'

'Oh.' Em's voice wobbled. 'I didn't know that. I'm sorry, Jooles. I just thought you didn't care, like you were ashamed of me. Didn't want to have anything to do with me.'

I reached my arm around her then and pulled her close. She was shivering, so I pulled my own scarf off and wrapped it across her shoulders. When she turned to say thanks, tears were trickling down her cheeks.

I don't know how long we sat there crying and holding each other before Em wiped her face on her sleeve and asked, 'Did you get any of my letters?'

'What? No!'

'So, where are they?'

We were both silent, wondering. I pulled out my hanky and wiped my face.

Em said, 'Did they even get posted? Has Mum got them? Or Dad? I bet it's Dad. He's still so angry with me.'

'But didn't you send them to my place? Not yours.'

Em sighed. 'Oh, yeah. It must have been someone at the Home then. We had to leave our letters on a table for someone to post. I hate that horrid place!'

'Oh, Em, I'm so sorry.'

We sat silent for a long time. I thought about all those moments we'd missed out on sharing—all those things she'd written and all the things I would have written.

'But Em, you know I'm always your best friend. Don't you? I mean, sure, I have other friends. If you came home, they'd be your friends, too.'

Her eyes glowed soft now. 'Thanks, Jooles,' she whispered. 'Thanks.'

I forced myself to ask her what had been burning in my mind ever since I found out she was having a baby. 'Em, what happened?'

Em looked out over the dam. She tugged at a weed growing out of the wall until it came away with a satisfying ripping sound. She pulled her sloppy jumper over her knees and hugged her legs. Then she glanced back at me before looking across the dam once more.

Finally, she said, 'I guess I just got lost. I listened to what other people said and believed them. Or I didn't, and tried to show them they were wrong about me.

'You know what Justin said about us in Intermediate? That followed me to Adelaide. I wanted to prove him wrong. And everyone who believed him.' Her voice was bitter. 'Well, I guess I did, huh?'

'Oh, Em…'

'I didn't even get to see my baby…' She hugged her legs even tighter and rested her forehead on her knees. She rocked back and forth. Perhaps she was weeping.

I didn't know what to say. I thought about Mrs Friend's Bible verses that helped me see what God thought about me. But how could I say that to Em? I think right then she hated God. Hated the people who took her baby. Hated her life.

We sat in silence for so long it got weird. It used to be we could hang out and not say anything and it would be fine. Comfy, even. But this was awkward. Maybe she was wondering what I thought of her now. And if she'd told me too much. I was starting to shiver, and my backside was getting numb from the cold concrete.

Suddenly, Em lifted her head and said, 'So, you and Jase?'

Straight away, the kisses came to mind. I blushed.

Em poked me. 'Come on, tell all.'

I felt shy. *Why is this so hard? This is Em, my best friend. Oh, yeah* and *Jase's twin.* I cleared my throat. 'Yeah. I reckon he's my new pair of jeans.'

Her face was blank. I tried to jog her memory. 'You know, not a second-hand pair?'

Finally, there was this little spark in her eyes and, hooray, she actually chuckled. 'Oh, yeah! Not soft and saggy in the bum!'

I asked Mum, 'How do you know you're in love?'

Mum's hands paused mid-air. Egg dripped off the fish onto the breadcrumbs. The Look appeared on her face. The corners of her mouth twitched. *Did I say something funny? I'm being serious!* 'I'm serious, Mum. How do you know? How did you know you were in love with Dad?'

Mum cleared her throat like she was stifling a laugh. Her eyes were shiny. 'Oh, love.' She dropped the fish back into the egg and wiped her hands and her eyes on her apron (the blue gingham with navy ricrac braid from the Guild trading stall). 'I don't know how to say. I just knew. You just know, somehow.'

Then she went on talking about being friends first, and having things you like to do together, and being complementary and complimentary, too. But I didn't hear much of that because I was thinking about Jase and did I just know? It was too confusing, too unsettling.

Then Mum said, 'But I know this, Julie. God's preparing the right one. Trust Him and you'll meet him at the right time.'

She turned back to the fish, and I heard her mumble under her breath, 'If you haven't already.' At least, I think that's what she said.

Chapter Thirty-Eight

We were at Girls Group. Mrs Friend had made gingernuts and we were dunking them and sucking the tea out of them. It was a competition to see who didn't lose all their biscuit in the tea. I lost, for sure. Mine went first and I had this gingery tea with soggy biscuit at the bottom. Not so bad, really.

Mrs Friend quietened us down and started to read from the Bible—a story about a woman called Hannah who didn't have kids, so she went to the temple and prayed. The priest thought she was drunk. Bit strange, I thought. Really? I mean, I've seen drunk people and I've seen people praying. Anyway, Mrs Friend talked about how Hannah believed that God could do anything and kept pestering Him for a baby. And He gave her one. It sounded a bit like when the twins whine around Mum and she gives in, and they get a bikkie even though it's close to teatime. Mrs Friend talked about how we can have faith like that—faith that believes God can do anything.

But then Suzy asked, 'Do you want to have kids, Mrs Friend?'

Everyone went so quiet I could hear the rustle of Gracie's shirt as she sat back against the couch. My tummy gurgled. The silence was awkward. Everyone knew—well apparently everyone except Suzy—that the Friends didn't have kids and were now getting a bit old to have them.

Mrs Friend's face had gone pale and sad. She sucked in her breath. Then she said very quietly, 'We would have liked to have a family, but we weren't blessed in that way. But I have all of you!' she added brightly.

Her face was still sad, like we really didn't make up for not having kids of her own. And I got that. I couldn't imagine Mum and Dad pretending that John and Christine from next door were their own kids. Part of why they loved us was because we were part of them. They made us—a thought I quickly tried to suppress because I felt my cheeks getting hot.

So, didn't Rev and Mrs Friend have enough faith? I didn't think that was right—they were ministers, after all.

I thought about Em and babies that were adopted and I wondered if Rev and Mrs Friend ever considered that. I mean, wouldn't adoption be like having your own kids? Or would it? Or would that be not having enough faith? I was confused.

I asked Mum once if I was adopted. She looked at me funny and laughed. Then she got a photo of her when she was my age. For real, it looked like I was looking at myself.

Anyway, Mrs Friend cleared her throat and Suzy had the good grace to look sorry for asking, and we went on with the Bible study.

LATER, when I told Mum what Suzy had asked Mrs Friend, she was aghast. 'What? That's very private! You never ask a lady that! Poor Kathryn! What did she say?'

'That God never blessed them with kids.'

Mum was quiet awhile.

'It's hard to understand, isn't it? Here's us with nine. Then there's babies that weren't planned for…'

I could tell she was thinking about Em's baby. I was, too, and tears pricked behind my eyes. My arms ached to hold Em's baby. And her.

EM DID COME HOME.

Mum said she had to go to town anyway, so she'd keep Mrs Price company. I wondered why Mum often had to go to town for doctors' appointments, but the anticipation of Em's homecoming soon put that out of my mind.

Whereas her mum had barely noticed Em in the past, she now spent more time with her, helping her with her schoolwork so she could catch up. Em said sometimes her mum would come and sit on the end of her bed and they'd talk about anything and everything. Mrs Price even told her secrets about her younger days, things she said she'd never told her own mum. And now she hugged Em good morning and kissed her goodnight.

But they never talked about what happened in Adelaide.

Her dad ignored her. He still felt the shame of Em's pregnancy. Not that many people knew. But I guess because he knew, it burned in him.

PART VIII
EMILY

Chapter Thirty-Nine

Term 3

Going back to Yarralinga High was the hardest thing I've ever done. Well, no. But it was up there.

Mum had coached me all through the last part of Term 2 and the September holidays. She was brilliant, getting work from the teachers for me and then helping me with anything I'd missed. I'd never felt so close to Mum. Some nights she came into my room and sat on my bed, and we talked. She'd never done that before. I wonder if she felt guilty, that in some way she was responsible for me getting pregnant. You know, not telling me the facts of life properly, not warning me. Or not paying me enough attention and listening to my struggles.

I could tell sometimes that she really wanted to talk about everything that happened to me, but she didn't, and so I didn't.

That first day of Term 3, Jooles came by our place to

walk with Jase and me. I was so glad of them, my front line of defence, one on each side as we went through the school gates. I was terrified that the news had got out or that someone had started rumours that were, inadvertently, the truth.

It started as soon as we got to the Matric home room. Candy and Co were at their lockers turning their dresses over at the waist and tying another belt on top to make them shorter. Giggling and glancing over shoulders at the boys by the bubblers. Skye spotted me first and nudged Candy.

She turned and said, 'Well, look who's back! Emily Price!'

I said nothing. Just went to find my locker next to Jooles's. But heat was creeping up my neck. My throat tightened and my heart started to pound.

Candy, sing-songy, 'What happened, Emily? Not good enough after all? Too slooooow?'

Jase turned to Candy then. 'Get lost, Candy.'

Candy's eyes widened in mock surprise. 'Oooo, the boy speaks.'

'Oooo,' chimed the Co.

Jase closed his locker and stood near me. Lorrie Schwartz was almost drooling over him. The biggest crush ever. *Not gunna happen!*

Jooles said quietly, 'Ignore her, Em. Don't waste your breath,' and calmly, slowly sorted what she needed for English and maths and closed her locker.

But Candy was on a roll. 'Gotcha girlfriend home, Julie?'

'Oooo, nice!' sang the backup.

Jooles said nothing.

'Anyways, Emily, why'd you come home before you finished? Why'd you even come home? I can't *wait* to get outa here!'

The Co all nodded.

We left them gaggling about leaving Yarralinga and headed in to Mrs Newman and Macbeth.

Jooles was different at school now. Tougher. More sure of herself. I wondered if that was because she and Jase were an item now—my best friend and my brother together… pretty cool! Or was it because of the Girls Group (surely they could've come up with a better name)? Maybe it was both, seeing Jase was in the Boys Group.

Anyway, I was glad how she seemed to shrug off Candy and Co's slights, except the times when they went for me and Jase wasn't around. Then she pushed back with some phrases that made Candy smirk and waltz off with her troupe in tow. Usually though, Jooles just steered us away. We avoided them as best we could—a bit hard when most of us were doing the same subjects.

WE WERE GOING over some homework together in my room (much too noisy at Jooles's house) trying to drum trigono-metric equations into our heads when neither of us found maths easy. I was struggling, big time. Mum came in with a cup of tea and some Anzacs. She leaned over and kissed the top of my head before she went. Tears pricked my eyes.

Jooles said, 'You've got the sweetest mum.'

'Mmm,' I agreed, not daring to try my voice with words.

'She really loves you, you know.'

At that, I couldn't hold the tears in any longer and blubbered till my nose was snotty and my face blotchy. Jooles just sat there quietly and patted my shoulder. Like a mum.

'I dunno if I can do this…' I sputtered.

'Do what?' she asked.

'You're good, Jooles. Just good, you know. You haven't gone off the rails like me. I've been so stupid. Ruined everything… I dunno what to do, if I can pass exams… what to do after school… all that…'

'Oh, Em.'

I didn't expect her to have an answer. It was enough that she still liked me and hung out with me. And stuck up for me. And listened. And got me a hanky out of my undies drawer. A truly good friend. I blew my nose loudly. 'Thanks.'

Jooles said, 'Look, Em, come to Girls Group with me tomorrow, yeah?'

She saw I looked ready to say, 'No thanks!' and hurried on, 'I'd really like you to. The girls are great—you know they are. Mrs Friend is the best. You wouldn't have to do anything, say anything. Just sit and listen. And we have the best suppers, too. Please come with me. Please.'

Oh-oh, she was starting to plead. I held up my hands in surrender. 'Alright! Fine. I'll come. Just this once.'

Jooles whooped and leaned across to hug me. 'Lizzy and I'll come by so we can walk together. Six-thirty. Yeah?'

I laughed. She'd planned it all that I'd say yes.

Liz and Jooles knocked right on six-thirty. Jase answered, of course. Anything to get in a quick kiss. Smoochy-cute, those two. He was off to his group, guitar case in hand. 'See you tomorrow,' he said to Jooles as he trotted out the gate.

She giggled and watched him till he turned the corner.

Lizzy looked at me and rolled her eyes. We grinned at each other.

'Ready?' she asked. 'Come on, dreamer.' She dragged Jooles back from la-la land and we headed over to the manse.

PART IX

JOOLES

Chapter Forty

It was so good that Em was home, and that she came to Girls Group, and that she laughed so much she said her belly hurt. Gracie, Liz, Rosie and Suzy welcomed her as if she'd always been part of us. She didn't join in the discussion—no one expected her to. But I know she listened when Mrs Friend asked Lizzy to tell us about her great-aunt Tabby who, even though her little girl had died in a horrible accident, learned to forgive and became the sweetest person ever.

Em was quiet as we walked her home to her gate. 'Thanks for taking me,' was all she said.

Lizzy asked, 'Come again?'

'Maybe. Yeah, I think so.' Em smiled. 'Night!' She ran up the path and disappeared into her house.

Jase, and sometimes Em, came over a lot on Saturday mornings (their dad was at the shop until lunchtime) and sometimes Mrs Price came and spent the morning with Mum in the kitchen, baking for the coming week. We worked with Dad in the garden while the little kids yahooed around the yard.

Patrick, Sean and Conal, who used to head off to the lake on Saturday mornings, had started hanging around home more. Actually, they hung around Jase and vied for his attention. 'Look what I found!' as they held up a witchety grub. They mimicked his every move or tried to impress him by chasing the squealing girls with worms.

Kathleen and Maria followed Jase, too, and when we all sat on the lawn for morning tea, they leant against his legs as if he belonged to the family. To them.

Pied Piper, Dad called him.

Brigid was the only one who preferred Em to Jase. She was nearly two but still tiny—she ate like a spoggy. She adored Em. I watched them play together with Brigid's dolly and pram and saw how good, yet hard, it was for Em. I'm sure it made her think about her own baby and wonder where it was and what it would be doing now. I hated thinking of the baby as 'it', but Em didn't even know if it was a girl or a boy.

I thought a lot about Em's story and how she was getting to know God. Even though she didn't say much in Girls Group, I could tell she was listening. Later, she'd ask me questions when we were together, questions I tried to answer but wished she'd ask Mrs Friend.

Sometimes, I felt like I was a second-rate Christian though I wished I didn't. I looked along the Friends' bookshelf and saw titles of people's true stories about how they'd done some rotten stuff, but then met Jesus and became totally different. I could see that was happening for

Em. One day, I hoped, she'd be free from that part of her past, too.

But where did that leave me? I didn't have any gutter-to-glory story. I didn't even want to go off the rails.

Mrs Friend said, 'Julie, do you suppose that perhaps the fact that you haven't abandoned your upbringing is evidence that God's been there all through your life? Keeping you safe? You don't have to have a big, messy story to show that God is real and loves you. Just keep on track, my dear.'

I sighed. Relieved. But where did that leave Em? What about her upbringing and God protecting her?

But then, I guess it's not all up to God, is it?

* * *

Mrs Friend had started a women's Bible study group at the end of Term 2. Mum joined them even though Granny and Pop Murphy rumbled a bit about it not being 'true religion' and 'what was the world coming to?' But as Mum pointed out, Roman Catholic services were changing too, and were much easier to understand since Father O'Day had been replaced by Father Flynn who used English liturgy instead of dead Latin.

Mum convinced our neighbour Lily to go to Bible study with her. And then, in Term 3, Lily was a special guest at our Girls Group.

Mrs Friend thanked her for coming and said, 'Now, girls, I've asked Lily if she would tell us some of her story.'

I could tell Lily was really nervous—she'd worn her hair in a sideways loose plait so that it partly covered the right side, the scarred side of her face, and she kept winding the plait around her fingers then smoothing it with the flat of her hands. Hands that were shaking.

Mrs Friend noticed too. She said, 'But first, let's play a couple of games.' She had Lily giggling and laughing with all of us, as we rolled the dice and ate as much chocolate with a knife and fork as we could before the next person rolled a six. I'm not sure, but I reckon Em was deliberately trying to *not* cut the chocolate. Finally, the block was gone and we drank cups of tea to wash it down.

Mrs Friend looked enquiringly at Lily who looked relaxed and warm from laughing. She nodded. And began to speak.

Chapter Forty-One

I think that I was the only one who'd heard her story before, and I only knew the bare bones—the car accident that killed her parents and caused her to be deaf in the right ear, and the fire that disfigured her. I knew about the grandparents who took her in and a little about meeting Hans at art school.

Lily told us briefly about these external things and then began to talk about what happened inside her afterwards. About her anger toward her parents for being killed (I could tell by everyone's faces we all struggled with that— *but it wasn't their fault!*). Lily must have known we'd think that because straight away she said, 'It wasn't reasonable but it was the way I felt… abandoned, alone.'

Then there was the anger toward the drunk driver for killing her parents. I remembered Mum's question, 'How *do* you forgive someone for something like that?' Rhetorical, but not. That was how we'd treated it because we didn't know.

And how she was angry at God for taking her parents, and not protecting them all.

And how she kept thinking, if only we'd not gone out that night, if only we'd left a bit later, if only… if only… if only…

'I was a mess. My grandparents didn't know what to do other than try to keep me going to school and doing usual everyday things. They were grieving, too. It's hard to help others when you are broken yourself. I hardly ate, lost a lot of weight, didn't have the energy or desire to do anything much.

'I had a beautiful art teacher in school. She let me do whatever I wanted rather than stick to the curriculum, and so I spent nearly all my lunchtimes in the art room. What I painted wouldn't have won any prizes, but it helped me inside.' Lily smiled at a thought. 'Before you ask, no, I don't have those paintings anymore. I've painted new work over every one of them.'

We collectively let out the breath we'd been holding while intent on every word. Em had been leaning forward, her hands clutched together in her lap. She seemed to come to herself and sighed as she settled back into the couch cushions.

'It seemed natural to go on to art school. Hans started that year, too. I liked him from the first time I spotted him. He always seemed to have this confident, peaceful way about him. And he was easy on the eyes.'

We were all smiling now. We loved a good romance story. We nodded, *go on*.

'But I was so shy. I mean, school had been really hard with

all the staring and teasing.' Lily indicated her face. 'It was probably the biggest reason I stayed hidden in the art room. There was no way I would push myself forward, especially with the girls that hung around Hans like butterflies on flowers. Anyway, in the end it was Hans who approached me.'

Gracie lifted her shoulders and let them drop as she giggled softly. Suzy's eyes were shining. Liz poked Rosie with her elbow and they both grinned. I felt that glow inside like when I thought of Jase.

'Well, there's more to it than that, but...'

We all groaned, 'Ohhhh!'

Mrs Friend stopped us with, 'Now, girls, Lily is right. She wants to tell us about something else as well. Maybe you can ask her about their romance another time.' She looked at Lily to continue.

'What I really wanted to tell you about was that I had to learn how to forgive, especially the drunk driver. I was twisted up inside about that. Even after five years, I was still having nightmares. I found it hard to control my temper—little things would make me lash out in anger. And I plotted to get revenge if I could find out where he lived. It's what unforgiveness does. We might think it hurts the other person, but in the end it hurts us.

'The short version is that Hans invited me to a church group on campus. I went with him, found the most wonderful group of friends, and met Jesus. I learned that forgiveness is a journey, one step at a time. Every time I thought of that night and that man or had a nightmare or my mind ran away with vengeful thoughts, I prayed, 'Jesus, help me to forgive him. I forgive him.' I didn't really feel any different, but over time the nightmares eased and I found I could focus on other things better.

'Then one day, as I was coming out of school, there was a man waiting at the bus stop. I recognised him straight away from the newspaper images of our accident. The drunk driver. He didn't know me. I just stood there watching him until the bus came, he boarded and was gone.

'Do you know what? I didn't feel anything toward him except pity. Not anger. Not revenge. Just pity for what his life must have been like after that horrible night.'

Silence.

We dared not break it with words or movement. The mantle clock tick-ticked. Mrs Friend bowed her head. We did the same. She asked us to think of someone we needed to forgive and invited us to begin the journey by taking a step.

Silence.

Em reached out her hand and touched mine. She sniffed softly. I heard the soft swish of her other hand brushing away tears from her cheeks. Was she thinking of Justin and Candy and their friends, too? And the baby's father? Herself?

Then Mrs Friend thanked Jesus for helping Lily to forgive and find peace, and asked Him to do the same for us.

'Amen,' we agreed.

Chapter Forty-Two

Em was doing fine at school, getting good grades for her assignments and classwork. She'd worked hard to catch up and it was paying off. Both her Mum and Jase helped her a lot.

One Saturday, mid-term, we were lounging on the back lawn with morning tea. Mum said she was just going to have a bit of a lie-down and could we watch the kids. She did look tired. I guess looking after the nine of us was getting a bit much. She'd come off a couple of committees so she could have more time at home. But still, maybe she needed to stop more.

I was braiding Kathleen's red curls while she and Maria leaned against Jase's legs. We all watched Em cradling Brigid's dolly while Brigid fed it with a toy bottle of milk. Over and over again, Brigid puzzled about the disappearing and reappearing magic milk. Kathleen turned to look at me and smiled the smug smile of the wise and knowing.

Suddenly, Em said, 'I've decided I'm going to do what Jase is. Sports teaching.'

I wasn't that surprised.

'If I get high enough marks to get in.'

'You will,' said Jase. 'Look at what you've done this term. Sure you'll get in. Anyway, Dad says they need lots more teachers now.'

I smiled. I knew he didn't mean that just *anyone* could get in at the moment, but it could be taken that way. Maybe I could get into college. Did I want to, though? Be a teacher?

Em said, 'Thanks.' She knew what Jase meant. To me, 'Aunty Sue and Uncle Steve won't take boarders anymore after me and Larry. Don't blame them. So, we might try to flat together if we can get jobs. Or go into a share house if we find the right people.'

I was glad of that. Jase would protect Em.

Brigid took her dolly back from Em, lifted it to her shoulder and patted its back.

'You're a good little mummy, Bridgy-didge,' said Em. Brigid glowed.

Dad called from the cabbages. 'Back to work, you lazy loafers! Smoko's over!' And we did.

So, what *was* I going to do with my life? So many of my classmates were applying for uni. So many going away. Em was. Jase was. He said, 'I gotta go, Jooles. It's the only way to do it.'

'Yeah, I know.' *What about me? Yeah, well that's stupid. It's not about me, is it? God, what do I do?* I wanted to say, 'My

Love Must Wait' but Jase wouldn't have a clue what I was talking about. *Would he?*

'What about you, Jooles?' asked Jase. 'Have you decided yet?'

I did. Right then. 'Teaching, I reckon. Probably English and history. Mrs Newman says I have a knack for it.'

'So good!' said Em. 'We could flat together!'

Jase grinned.

I talked it over with Mum that maybe I'd go to Adelaide and study after all… teaching English and history.

She said, 'You're not doing this because of Jason and Emily are you? Do you really want to train for teaching? It's got to be about what you want for your life, Julie.'

Well, yeah. I wanted to be with Jase. But I knew she meant for me to do something apart from that. Have a job like she never had.

'Yes, I want to train for teaching.'

'Good. Good then. We'll need to talk to your father about going guarantor for your bond.'

I looked blank.

'It's what the government requires: in case you don't teach as long as you study. Then you have to pay back the money you owe. Dad would have to pay it if he's guarantor.'

'Oh,' I said. 'Well, I won't let that happen!' No way was I going to let them down like that.

And that was it. My path set out before me.

PART X
EMILY

Chapter Forty-Three

J ase told me that all through that year, Candy and Co had kept taunting Godfrey, the Maud Springs Kid, but he'd just kept to himself and seemed not to notice. They were still at it in Term 3. I cringed every time I heard their digs—every stabbing word twisted in me. I still lived in fear of them finding out about my baby. My longing for her (I always thought of my baby as 'her') was a big, heavy hole in my gut. How could a hole be heavy? I dunno. But it was.

We were back in home class at the end of the day. Our demountable was an oven in an early November heatwave. The fans, out of balance, clicked annoyingly and did nothing to cool us. Blowflies droned along the windows. Mr Blake was droning information about the soon-to-be matric exams—what rooms, what times, what to bring—when Mr Thomas, the headmaster, tapped on the open door. 'I need to talk to the students when you've finished, thanks Paul.'

Mr Blake nodded and wrapped up. Mr Thomas stood

before us and cleared his throat. Of course, we were all trying to guess who was in trouble this time. Had they found out who'd stuffed the potato in Mr Newman's exhaust pipe? Or who'd lifted Miss Daly's Mini into a tight parking space so she couldn't get it out. Or who'd used line marker to draw a giant rude sign on the lawn of the oval. (It was getting near the end of school and the boys were fidgety with the stresses of study.)

Whatever it was, Mr Thomas was not happy. Actually, he looked sad rather than angry.

'Boys and girls, I have some very bad news, I'm afraid.' He cleared his throat again and his Adam's apple bobbed up and down as he swallowed. The home siren blared, but no one dared move. 'I've had a call from the police in Port Pirie (someone gasped) to say that Godfrey Young was found dead this morning.'

At that, the room erupted with cries of disbelief—What? No way? Really? Heck! How? What happened, sir?

Sir waited for us to quieten. 'It appears that the young man took his own life.'

No! No way! Why?

'There was a note…' He stopped. Realised that he shouldn't have revealed that.

What'd it say?

'Even if I knew what it said, I would not be at liberty to say. If any of you can shed some light on why Godfrey may have done this, please, my door is open.

'We will let you know when the funeral is to be. I'm sure the parents would appreciate your attendance and, of course, we will give you time from school to do so if necessary. Meanwhile, I hope it won't keep you from preparations for your examinations. I am sorry be the bearer of bad news. Thank you, Mr Blake.' And he was gone.

Mr Blake looked as stunned as we felt. He nodded and said, 'Good afternoon, students,' without the usual cheeriness that showed he was glad it was the end of another school day.

We gathered our things and shuffled through the door. At the lockers, a boy murmured, 'Couldn't take you-know-who anymore, I reckon,' and heads turned toward Candy and Co. She had her head in her locker, then she clanged the door shut, latched her satchel and walked out with her face tight and red. Chin high. Eyes ahead. Lips pursed.

Lorrie and Skye followed suit.

NEARLY ALL THE class attended Godfrey's funeral; Candy and Co were conspicuous by their absence. True to his word, Mr Thomas gave us time off even though matric exams were fast approaching. They bussed us to Maud Springs.

We hung by the church gate like wide-eyed sheep in the abattoir holding pen, a tight group unsure how to act. Very few of us had been to a funeral before. We followed our teachers to seats at the back. Outside was torrid, but inside was cold as a tomb. The atmosphere was so heavy that we were subdued, oppressed to silence, but the sound of Godfrey's family mourning will stay with me forever.

We didn't go to the graveside. Mr Mullins ushered us to the bus and drove us back to school. Godfrey's vacant seat stared at us accusingly.

REV AND MRS FRIEND had a special combined meeting for our groups to help us with Godfrey's death. Even kids who didn't usually attend came along. I guess we all wanted answers and hoped that the Rev and Mrs Friend would be able to give them.

I kept remembering Adelaide, how alone I'd felt, how nothing seemed to work for me or ever would, like I was right at the bottom of a deep pit with no way out and no light. Was that how Godfrey had felt? Worse, I think. Couldn't fight anymore. No one to fight for him.

Rev Friend opened the time by asking if anyone had questions.

Everyone wanted to ask, Why? But no one wanted to be first.

So, I did.

And then everyone jumped in with ideas, opinions, things that their parents had said. And more questions. Could we have stopped him? Done something about Candy and Co? Or was there something else that made him do it? Rev and Mrs Friend mostly let us talk but every now and then commented in a kind and helpful way.

Then Tom asked, 'Will he go to heaven?'

Conversation stopped. Eyes turned to the Rev.

'What are you thinking, Tom?' he asked.

Tom swallowed, suddenly uncomfortable as if he'd asked a forbidden question. But he said softly, 'Well, suicide is killing, isn't it? And murderers don't go to heaven, do they? It says so in the Bible.'

'Mmm. It also says that everyone who calls on the name

of the Lord will be saved. We can't know what happens between a person and God in the moments before they die. Perhaps, he called on Jesus to save him. We can only hope that he did.

'There is so much we don't know. But this I do. Never stop trusting that God has you in His care. Even if you find yourself in a place where it seems there is no way out, God can help you find one.'

Had he read my mind? Did he know what I had done to get myself out?

'God will always open a way. Never stop trusting him. Now, let me pray for us.'

Rev Friend led us in a prayer asking God to accept Godfrey, and about us repenting for anything we might have done wrong or didn't do to help him. There was a lot of quiet sobbing and nose blowing as he finished. Even the boys.

FOR THE REST OF TERM, Candy and Co were as subdued as we had been at the funeral. They barely talked to anyone. They didn't come to the end of year dinner-dance. As soon as exams were over, Candy disappeared—someone said she was working in the pub for her dad. But we never saw her around. Lorrie stayed away—she said her mum needed her to help with cooking for the harvesters. Skye kept coming but stayed by herself, a lonely figure among those excited to be finishing high school.

AND THEN, the end. Not just for the year, but forever! We passed out the school gates for the last time, whooping and laughing and chanting, 'No more homework, no more books, no more teachers' dirty looks,' like we used to do in primary school.

There was a sense of finality, the end of childhood, of freedom from routines and being told what to do… for a while anyway. We'd done all we could and now could enjoy the deliciousness of no timetables… until matric results came out in late January.

PART XI
JOOLES

Chapter Forty-Four

Mum went to another appointment in Adelaide in the week before Christmas. A couple of days later, I heard her crying in their bedroom. Dad was still at work. I stood outside wondering if she didn't want anyone to hear and that's why the door was shut. Wondering if I should knock. If I should go in. I raised my hand, but then let it drop. Dad'd be home soon. He could go in and talk to her.

I went to the kitchen and started peeling the potatoes for tea.

Dad and Mum called me, Patrick, Sean and Conal into the sitting room after the other kids were in bed. Mum's eyes were still red-rimmed. She looked so sad. She hadn't said anything during teatime, not even to tell Conal off for taking Kathleen's last piece of sausage. Even when Kathleen screamed at him.

We sat lined up along the couch, me in the sagging middle with my brothers falling against me on either side, poking each other and giggling.

Mum and Dad sat in their chairs opposite. Still and quiet.

It was hot. The sitting room faced west and the sun still shone low over the hills. The boys smelt sweaty. My mind was racing with what Mum and Dad were going to say. Was it about Mum's crying?

The mantle clock chimed seven. Dad looked at Mum and leant forward to rest his elbows on his knees. He ran a hand through his hair.

'Kids, you know how Mum's not been feeling well for a while now, how she's had to go down to town for a few appointments?'

We nodded. I'm not sure that the boys had noticed, being so wrapped in their own worlds. But I did. I'd seen how tired she always seemed to be, how I'd find her asleep on her bed in the afternoons. Mum, the tireless, social whirly-whirly. Other things, too, like her clothes seemed to hang off her when once they fitted well. She wasn't eating much and I sometimes saw her wince and press her hand against her stomach.

Dad continued. 'Well, Mum's not well at all. The doctors say that she needs to be in hospital for a while. Maybe in Adelaide, not Redbank. We don't know how long it'll be for.'

'When?' I whispered.

Mum answered. 'I'm not sure yet. Maybe not until February. We'll have a wonderful Christmas first.' I could tell she was struggling to be upbeat, to not cry. Dad reached out and enclosed her hand in his. She stroked the back of his hand with her fingertips.

'When Mum comes home, she'll need lots of help. So, we need you all to look after each other. Help with the little kids. Can you do that?'

We nodded again. What could we say?

'Right,' said Dad. 'Off you go then. Bed.'

We rose slowly. The boys called, 'Night,' as they escaped the heaviness. I lingered. I wanted to know more. But I didn't. I wanted to ask. But I didn't want to hear the answers.

Mum lifted her hand out to me, and I went to sit on the floor and lean against her legs.

She stroked my hair. 'I'll be alright, Julie. Just a hiccup in life.'

Dad said softly, 'Fi, she needs to know.' He was crying. I'd never seen Dad cry before.

And they told me then, that it was a cancer.

And Mum could die.

———

I LAID on my back on my bed and stared at the dead insects in the plastic light shade, at a huntsman lurking in the corner, at a dark stain on the wall where I'd hit a mozzie after it'd bitten me. Mum was sick, really, really sick, and she could die. I thought of Godfrey's funeral, the coldness, the grieving, his empty chair, the space left. I felt unmoored. Treading water in a dark sea with nothing to hold onto. And I was sinking. My heart was wild. I gulped in breaths. And then out flooded, 'No! No! No! Mum can't die! I need her! God, you can't take my mum!'

Maria disturbed and whimpered. I tried to muffle my sobs in my pillow. Then Mum was there, anchoring me to her. And the darkness slowly ebbed away.

Chapter Forty-Five

Mum and Dad tried to explain it to the younger kids. Kathleen and Maria clung to each other and wouldn't let Mum out of their sight. She got cross at them when they kept getting under her feet, tripping her up. 'I can't see you all the time!' she said, exasperated. She scored a lot of bruises on her arms and legs that Christmas.

I heard the twins talking to Brigid.

'They put mummies in a oesophagus,' said Aiden, knowledgeably.

'And their insides go up to heaven,' added James.

Brigid started singing, 'Heaben is mmmm pace...'

'That's not how it goes!' said Aiden and began to correct her. 'Heaven is a won'erful place, filled wiv...'

I didn't want to think about heaven and Mum seeing her saviour's face.

I left them to it.

I think that telling Jase and Em about Mum was one of the hardest things I'd ever done. Not just because Mum was so sick that she could die, but for what it would mean for me. For us.

I was afraid. I wanted desperately to go to Adelaide, to be close to both Jase and Em. To prove to myself that I could exist outside of Yarralinga, that I could be a good teacher. But what about Mum? What about Dad, if Mum… And the kids. And me. Could I live with myself if I went?

I decided and I was sure about what I had to do—to not go to teachers college but stay home and help look after my family. We didn't know if Mum would be alright. We didn't know how the surgery or the treatment would affect her. There was so much we didn't know, couldn't know. God knew. I asked Him all the time. But He wasn't telling.

I told Jase and Em together, sitting on the back lawn under the almond tree. It felt a bit easier that way. I watched their eyes, so alike, widen in disbelief. I guess like mine had done when Mum and Dad told me.

They were both quiet, and then Em said, 'Oh, Jooles, I'm so sorry.'

I misted up and hung my head. 'Yeah.'

Jase scooted over next to me and put his arm around my shoulders. Snug. Comforting. I leant into him. He kissed the side of my forehead.

My throat constricted. 'And,' I croaked, 'I've decided I can't go to Adelaide after all.'

'Oh,' said Em.

I felt Jase slowly nod his head, but he still said nothing.

We sat for a while in silence. A flock of spoggies flew through the almond tree with a whoosh of wings. A couple of chooks scratched around the veggies, pock-pocking as they searched for bugs.

'It's the right thing,' said Jase. 'It's best you stay with your family.'

'Yeah,' said Em. 'It is.' Trying to convince herself. Trying to make it easier for me and my decision. 'I hope your mum'll be okay. And maybe you can come the next year.'

'Yeah. Maybe.'

I WENT DOWN to Swanton Hair and talked to Nina McCarthy about hairdressing. She was rinsing the perm solution out of Mrs Hunter's hair. Doc and Mrs Hunter were retired, but rather than staying in Redbank near the hospital they'd chosen to live in quieter Yarralinga. She had her hair done at Swanton's every week.

'Well, hairdressing's been good for me,' said Nina. 'Fits in around looking after my girls. And I get to talk a lot.' She laughed. 'My skill! And I do love people and making them look good with a nice hairstyle. They come in here feeling tired and down, and go out on top of the world.' She guffawed again—Nina laughed as much as she talked. I loved the loud, free sound that occasionally ended in a snort. It made me want to laugh, too.

Mrs Hunter's voice floated up from the basin. 'So true. So true. Feel like a million dollars.'

'Tell you what, how about you come down a few Saturday mornings and watch and learn and see if you like it? Tee it up with your mum and dad first, of course.'

'Umm, sure, that'd be great. But can I come some week-days instead? Bit busy on Saturday mornings.'

'Ah,' she said. 'Righto. How about this Wednesday coming?'

'That'd be great. I'll talk to Mum.'

'So sorry about your mum,' said Nina.

Mrs Hunter said, 'They're getting good results with treatment these days, dear.'

'Oh, ok. Thanks.'

I stood there, not sure whether to stay and watch, or go, when Nina spoke again, 'So, how's that Price boy treating you, then?' Left field.

I flushed. Was everyone watching us? I stumbled a reply, 'Good. Yeah, good.'

'Good,' echoed Nina. 'You're worth taking care of, you know. Make sure you remember that.'

Mrs Hunter was up from the basin and heading to the chair. 'And so is he, young lady. Make sure you take good care of him, eh?' And I heard her grumble something about 'too much hanky-panky these days' as she lowered her large form into the chair.

'Yes, Mrs Hunter,' I said meekly and nodded my goodbyes.

When I told Mum what I was thinking, she said, 'So, you're sure, Julie, that that's what you want to do?' There were tiny furrows between her brows. Was she trying to make me second-guess?

'Yes, Mum. That's what I want to do.' I said it as firmly as I could.

Her face softened, and she gathered me into a hug.

'Oh, my love. That's decided then. Thank you. I am glad

that I'll have my biggest girl home with me.' She rested her cheek against the side of my head. I could feel warm tears wetting my hair.

'Thanks, Mum.' And I realised how glad I was to be home with her.

Chapter Forty-Six

Dad took Mum to Adelaide for her surgery in early New Year.

Gramma and Grandpa Kent stayed with us, and Grandpa Kent went home during the day to care for his own garden. He'd come back looking really worn out, have a cuppa and a sandwich, then go outside to water Dad's veggies.

Granny and Pop Murphy brought meals. Mrs Price brought meals. Lots of people brought meals. We didn't cook much.

That January passed in a blur of people visiting—our house felt like Rundle Street.

Hans and Lily helped with the little kids and the garden.

Gracie's dad kept Dad's car filled with petrol because he knew how much it cost to drive to Adelaide all the time; Gracie's baby brother had spent a lot of time at the Children's Hospital in Adelaide soon after he was born. Dad'd helped a lot when Mr Burton was out of work, bringing veggies and helping him get the job at Yarralinga Farm Services and Garage. So, Mr Burton said he was glad to return the favour.

Mrs Friend brought roses from her garden. She prayed with me and gave me a bookmark with Psalm 23 on it. She'd underlined verse four. 'Read it every day, Julie,' she said.

Mrs Hawkins never came—I never expected her to. But surprise, surprise, Mrs Vincent dropped by once with a cake she'd baked. She stood at the front door offering it with, 'I hope your mum will be alright, Julie. I'm sorry,' before fleeing down the path, holding her hat in the hot afternoon wind. I wasn't sure if the 'sorry' encompassed our history as well.

I longed for Mum and Dad to be home again, for the quiet of just us.

I longed for before, when Mum was alright.

I prayed long.

Longing prayers.

I struggled to trust God, even with reading the scripture verse every day. I felt that we'd never get out of the valley of death's shadow. And sometimes, I couldn't see God in it.

I became a drill sergeant with the kids. I think they hated me that summer. I forced them to do nearly every-thing for themselves and rostered them on to all sorts of jobs like feeding the chooks and shutting them up, helping cook, cleaning the bathroom, making their beds, washing up, drying up, putting dirty clothes in the laundry…

Ordering the kids around felt like I had control over what was happening to us. Some control, at least.

Gramma sat me down one evening and told me to stop

taking it out on the kids. 'They're trying to find their own way with all of this, too, Julie. Give them a break. And give yourself a break.'

The next day, when Jase and Em came, Gramma ordered us to go swimming. 'Take her out of here! I want some peace and quiet.' She smirked. 'She bosses me around like you wouldn't believe!'

So, we rode out to the waterhole.

We swam a bit, then I'd hardly laid down on my towel when I was asleep. I didn't wake up until someone swung off the rope with a blood-curdling yell. I jerked and opened my eyes.

Jase was watching me, brown eyes smiling. 'Hiya,' he said.

Em was swimming again. I could see her chatting with Gracie and Liz.

'Hiya.' I yawned and stretched. 'How long was I asleep?'

'Oh, like a hundred years. I was just about to kiss you awake.'

I laughed. It felt so good to be away from the house. To be with Jase.

DAD CAME HOME WITHOUT MUM; she'd had her surgery and was staying with her sister, Aunty Deidre who was a nurse, to be close to the hospital for her radiotherapy.

Dr and Mrs Hunter came around. She sat at the kitchen table and asked Gramma how she was. I'd not heard Gramma talk about it before—I guess I was so wrapped up in my own feelings, I didn't think a lot about how others felt.

I left them to it and went to make sure the kids were tidying their rooms. Gramma said later that it was 'just the ticket—a good old cry'.

From the sleepout where the boys were making more mess than tidiness, I could hear Dr Hunter talking to Dad on the back veranda. Though retired, Dr Hunter said he kept up with his medical journal reading. He talked in comforting tones about the advancements in treatment these days.

Rev Friend spent lots of time with Dad. They didn't talk much, mostly sat and gazed over Dad's garden, and drank tea, or beers, depending on the time of day. Every now and then, Dad'd murmur something and the Rev would murmur in reply, too soft for me to make it out. But Dad always came in from those times looking lighter, more hopeful and more interested in what we were doing.

He sometimes came to me unexpectedly and held me to his chest and said, 'Thank you, girlie,' in a cracked kind of voice. 'Dunno what we'd do without you.'

PART XII
EMILY

Chapter Forty-Seven

January 1973

The day Matric results were due to come out, Jooles came by, and we trotted down to hang around the front door of Carey's Grocery with the rest of the matric class waiting for Dad to cut the strings on the *Advertiser* bundle.

We paced and sighed a lot. Fidgeted. Some chewed their fingernails. Some jogged up the path and back—I did. It's what calms me most. Liz kept saying, 'It'll be alright,' over and over. Most of the boys swaggered around nonchalantly, pretending that it was no big deal. But it was. This was the final releasing of school ties, the final tick for going on to tertiary study (or not). A reward for twelve years' hard labour. Had I done enough to catch up and get into teachers college?

Finally, Uncle Ken opened the doors. He faked surprise.

'What! What d'you lot want, then?' We swarmed in and bought up all the *Advertisers*, took them outside and, with shaking hands, discovered our fate.

Our names were there, next to our subjects and our grades. My heart sank. Emily Price. An 'E'! No, wait a minute that 'E' meant English! A 'B'. Phew, that's good. I read on. It was fine. I did fine. Two B's, two C's and a D for Maths (that'd be right). My nervousness drained away. I looked up to Jase then.

He was grinning at me. 'You did good, Em!'

He'd already seen my results and I hadn't looked at his. Straight B's. Wow! We both looked at Jooles. Her hair was hanging down hiding her face. Jase touched her on the shoulder. She jumped and looked up at him. Her eyes were wide and so was her mouth—the biggest O.

'What?' I looked for her name then. She'd got an A for English and three B's and a C for Maths. I dropped the paper on the ground and grabbed her hands and danced her around laughing. 'You could've got into teachers college!' slipped out before I realised what I'd said.

Jooles's face fell and her eyes watered.

'I'm sorry. So sorry! I didn't mean …' I grabbed her in a hug.

'It's alright,' she said and pulled away and smiled at Jase and me. 'You guys are going to get in easily!'

All over the footpath, there were little cries of shock, disbelief, disappointment, joy. A couple of the girls fled to their parents' cars in tears. Lorrie Schwartz was one. She passed the *Advertiser* to Candy Murphy who was sitting in her dad's car. Candy rolled up the window, found her name and swore so loudly we heard it through the closed glass. Her dad took off fast.

The other girls from Girls Group did well, too. Rosie got four A's and a B. Brainy! She said she was going to study law. Suze was still deciding to go to art college or into fashion, and Gracie, an Arts degree. Lizzy was going nursing, starting at Redbank Hospital in a few weeks.

So that was it. We soon received our acceptance to teachers college, and the rest of January and February went by in a blur of getting organised to go.

Yep, I was going back to Adelaide.

But this time, it was going to be different. I was different and I had Jase, my twin, my anchor, my best friend. Well, my equal best friend. I tried not to think too much about how I'd miss Jooles. And I tried not to talk about how excited I was in front of her, because I didn't want to make her feel bad about deciding to stay.

We hung around together as much as we could in those last weeks. Both Jase and I went over to the Kents often and helped with the little kids. Jooles's mum came home in February, though she had to go back to Adelaide sometimes for more check-ups and treatment. She looked thin and sick; her eyes were almost too big for her face. But she was upbeat and told us funny stories about people she'd met in hospital that made us laugh with her.

She said that she was going to beat this thing, God willing. Once, I came around the tank stand to find Mrs Friend holding Mrs Kent's hands. Both had their heads down and eyes closed, praying. I pulled up short and waited. It didn't seem right to interrupt, and I felt something holding me back from going close. Yeah, I reckon God was willing *and* could make her better.

And that was why I was different. I didn't only have Jase as my anchor. I had God... well, He had me. I knew who I was, and I was going to be just that.

PART XIII
JOOLES

Chapter Forty-Eight

February 1973

'Coming for a walk?' asked Jase as he looked at Em and me.

We'd finished tea at the Price's, and Mum and Dad had headed home after wishing Jase and Em all the best for the year in Adelaide.

Em looked at her mum. Then she looked at Jase and me. 'Nah, you go. I'll give Mum a hand to clean up.'

I hovered. Then I rushed to her and gave her the tightest hug I could. I was going to miss her so much. She hugged me back, the best friend-hug ever. We were both crying as we drew apart.

'Be home soon, Em,' I sniffed.

'Oh, yeah! As soon as this guy says, I'll be in the car like a shot!'

'This guy' was smiling from ear to ear. Dad had helped Mr and Mrs Price find a car for Em and Jase's birthday—an

EH Holden that had come into the Yarralinga Garage to be sold. It'd belonged to an old lady who only drove it to the shops once a week. Old, but reliable and in beautiful condition.

'Go on. Go,' said Em, shooing with her hands. 'See you in a couple of weeks.'

Without really thinking about it, Jase and I walked down Sturt Street, along Redbank Road and out to the dam wall. It was a familiar and, therefore, comforting route. We didn't talk. Just held hands and walked. When we reached the wall, I was about to sit and hang my legs over the edge when Jase turned in front of me and held both my hands. My stomach flip-flopped. He kissed me. We kissed.

I was suddenly afraid. I pulled away.

He looked hurt. Puzzled. 'What? What's wrong?'

'I need to know what colour your eyes are. What if I can't remember? What if I forget what you look like?'

There were smile lines at the corners of those warm brown eyes.

'Silly duffer!' he said and pulled me to his chest.

But I pushed back. I wanted to see into those eyes forever. 'Don't *you* forget *me*, will you?'

'No way!'

His grin was wide. 'You're the one for me, Jooles Kent.'

I sighed and let him draw me back in. 'And you for me, Jase Price.'

Epilogue

April 1977, ADELAIDE

I was in town for wedding shopping with Em. We found all the fabric and notions for her dress and mine, and makeup for us both after Em had sat for a trial at one of the makeup counters in David Jones. She looked wonderful. We laughed our way through lunch in Coles Cafeteria—she even ate a whole pasty—and talked wedding plans. She kept twiddling her engagement ring around her finger. I was so happy to see her so happy. She was loving teaching and that was where she'd met John. She told me that she and her dad were talking now, and he'd even agreed to walk her down the aisle.

She asked after Mum, and I was glad to be able to say that she was doing well. Better than the doctors had expected. A miracle, some said.

'Oh, Jooles, it's so good!' said Em. 'God is so good!'

'Yeah. Yeah, it is.' But we were always afraid they'd find

more cancer when Mum went for her check-ups. I'd wait with my stomach twisted up for Dad to call from Adelaide with news.

Just then, a mum walked past balancing a laden tray and towing a toddler who was clutching a scrap of rug to her cheek and sucking a thumb. She was only table height, dressed in a floral print frock with smocking across the chest. Her hair was dark and there was so much of it—more than I would have thought possible for such a tiny child. It was tied in two pigtails with pink ribbons. Her wide, dark eyes tracked me and then Em as she went past and was lost among the crowded tables.

I heard Em sigh. She was watching the place where the little girl had disappeared. Tears welled in her eyes.

'I told John,' she said. 'About the baby.'

I reached my hand across the table to squeeze hers. 'Was that alright?' I asked.

Her eyes overflowed as she said, 'I feel like I don't deserve how good he is to me. He said God's forgiven me, and he does too, and we're starting new.'

I nodded. *White for your wedding, Em. It's a brand-new beginning.*

'He said I need to forgive myself.' She looked at me fully.

Part of me wanted to laugh because her tears had made black mascara rivers down her cheeks. But I made The Look and said, 'Yes, Em, you do.' I ferreted around in my bag and found her a hanky.

'Ta,' she said and wiped her cheeks and eyes. 'I'm trying, Jooles. You know, like Lily said, it's a journey. But sometimes, I just wish it never happened. Will I ever stop regretting it?'

I didn't know.

We sat in silence for a while. Then suddenly, Em said, 'Shoes!' She looked at her watch. 'I've only got another hour. Come on!'

After she left to meet up with her John—smart, kind and totally head-over-heels in love with her—I had a couple of hours before heading down to the train station, so I strolled down North Terrace and into the Art Gallery to sit with Hans's Gratitude statue. She never ceased to give me joy. I walked around her and then sat on the bench gazing up at her beautiful motion caught in stone. The old, friendly security guard had been replaced with a younger, bored one who leant in the corner and gazed apathetically as people exclaimed over Dancing Lily (I liked to call her that now I knew Lily was the subject).

I sat and thought of Hans and Lily and Lily's growing tummy; they said they didn't mind if they had a boy or a girl as long as it was healthy. At Girls Group, which I now ran with Mrs Friend, we prayed that they'd have twins. Mrs Friend always finished with, 'Whatever you think's best for them, God.'

I thought that I'd like Jase and me to have twins one day. And, suddenly, I was missing him. I looked at my watch—still nearly two hours before I had to be at the station. I sighed. Since we'd been married, we'd hardly been apart. Well, not quite true—he was teaching in Redbank and had to leave early and usually wasn't back until late afternoon. Sometimes, he worked after tea to prepare lessons and mark papers. But we were together, the two of us in our cute little rental in Yarralinga, and I was so content.

I'd thought that the four years he was away studying in Adelaide would never end. He got home whenever he could, bringing Em with him, and sometimes I visited them in Adelaide. In between, we wrote long letters about anything and everything. I've kept them tied with ribbon in a box in our wardrobe. Then, finally, he'd graduated and we could be married. True to her promise, Mum bought me the fabric and pattern that I chose for my dress—no curtain material—and I had new shoes. Nina did my hair, but she wouldn't let me pay. Said it was a pleasure to do mine and Em's after all the hours I'd put in working with her.

Yes, of course, Em was my bridesmaid, just like I'll be hers.

Can you actually burst with happiness? I think I came close when I walked into the church on Dad's arm and there was Jase looking down the aisle at me, his grin wide and wonderful. He looked so hot in his suit! My stomach flip-flopped. My knees shivered. I suddenly remembered the Deb Ball, Jase meeting us at the gate, sparring with Dad about marrying his daughter, and I giggled. Dad patted my hand on his arm, and puffed his chest out even further. As we walked past Mum, I could see she was already weeping. She'd said to me, 'Don't worry about me, Julie, I always cry at weddings.' *God, I am forever grateful to you for healing her.*

And then Dad put my hand into Jase's and said, 'Look after her, son.'

To which Jase replied, 'I won't let her trip down them steps. Sir.' He winked at Dad.

I giggled, feeling like a treasured, sparkly jewel.

Dad chuckled and went to join Mum and the tribe squashed into the front pews.

The rest of the service is a blur in my memory. Jase's glowing eyes and the warmth of his hands holding mine, those are the things I remember most.

And as I sat there in the Gallery, I longed to be home with him. I looked at my watch again. Still an hour to kill. I got up, walked once around Dancing Lily and then out into the sunshine, across the road and into David Jones. Maybe, I could find a new lipstick for Mum.

I wandered and window shopped. I was coming out of John Martin's and glanced across Rundle Street and there she was. Candy Murphy. I would've known her anywhere, even though it'd been over four years. Her hair was still that gorgeous honey blonde and fell in waves to her waist. She was wearing a powder-blue pant suit that showed off her curves—yep, I bet there were lacy D-cups under that.

She was with a taller man, good-looking and dressed immaculately in a suit. The jacket was open. I could see a trim torso in a teal turtleneck. He was holding the handles of a pusher in which sat a blond child of around two, squirming and crying and trying to escape the restraint.

Candy must have felt my gaze on her because she looked up then and saw me. Her face blanched white and her mouth fell open a bit. Out of the blue, I thought, *Watch out for flies!*

Then she rested a hand on the man's arm, said something and turned back to me. She started walking across the street towards me. Was it my imagination or did the cars stop for her? I was rooted to the footpath, tensing myself for the caustic comments that would surely come out of that perfectly lipsticked mouth. She was beaming a wide smile of recognition. She lifted a hand in a twinkly wave.

'Julie Kent! Oh, Price, now, isn't it?' she exclaimed as she reached my side of the street. It was late afternoon, so this side was now in shadow. I shivered.

She gushed on, 'I don't believe it! Oh, it's so good to see you!' Then she stopped and dropped her eyes (bright blue eyeshadow, thick eyeliner and loads of mascara) and the colour of beetroot radiated from under her heavy makeup. 'Oh.'

I had no idea what to say. *You're the last person I want to see.* I looked at my watch—pointedly.

She noticed. 'You're catching the train home, then?'

'Mm-mm,' I mumbled. 'Just down for the day.'

She slid from foot to foot. Fiddled with the strap on her handbag. I'd just seen one like it in John Martin's, so I knew that it cost a lot. A real lot.

She found her voice then and looked up at me. She was very beautiful. No wonder the boys all had gone for her and—I glanced past her at the guy rocking the pusher back and forth—still did.

'Jooles, I… Argh, this isn't easy.' She slapped her hand on her cheek and ran it down to cradle her jaw. Her brow creased. 'Look, I really am glad to run into you like this. I didn't know what to do about it but, look, I'm really, really sorry for the way I treated you back in school. I know I was cruel and… I'm sorry…' she finished lamely as she watched me for a response. 'I mean, I don't want to make excuses, but I hated my life and…'

I held up my hand then. 'It's fine,' I said. I'd heard more about her horrible home-life since her parents had split, and her dad'd sold the pub and moved away. I knew in my head that I'd forgiven her, but my heart still hurt. Seeing her was reopening wounds. 'I forgive you. I do.'

At that, Candy clapped three times and opened her arms to pull me into a hug. I stood as stiff as a wooden doll and let her.

'Thank you! Thank you!' she cried. 'You've no idea how much that means to me.'

The sound of the kid's whinging hit the air waves then, strident above the sounds of cars and people. 'Wheel! Wheel!'

Candy's head snapped toward him. Then back to me. 'Look, I gotta go. We promised him a ride on Cox Foys' ferris wheel, and it'll be closed soon. And he's being a pain!' She smiled that winning-Miss-Australia smile, flicked her fingers in a wave and called, 'Hope it's not so long next time!' as she stepped across the street.

God, I forgive her. I do. I do. I know that one day my heart will catch up.

Like Lily's had. One day, I'd meet Candy out of the blue like this and not feel the past barbs. Maybe even feel sympathy. Maybe.